PAPERBACK VERSION
ISBN: 978-0-9908989-0-0
ISBN-10: 0990898903
FIRST EDITION

PUBLISHED BY: EDUCATED THUG PUBLICATION
COVER DESIGN: AMB Branding and Design

OMERTA
By: Hec Tha Plug

Chapter One
Don't Get Caught

A light mist fell from the night's summer sky as Anthony "Pretty Tony" Johnston raced up the boulevard at over seventy miles per hour in his black BMW 745i. The interior of the luxury vehicle reeked of high-grade marijuana, and the bag of dope and handgun in his possession were surely enough to put him away for life, if the cops pulled him over and charged him as a repeat offender.

Although he was young and rich, Pretty Tony definitely couldn't afford to be pulled over, so he still didn't slow down. Young Jeezy was performing in concert at the concert hall and Pretty Tony just had to make it there to support him. Pretty Tony idolized Young Jezzy for his authenticity and realness. Jeezy could've offered substantial assistance to federal agents trying to implicate him in BMF's alleged drug activity, but Jezzy stood firm. He honored the principles of Omerta and kept pursuing his rap career. In Pretty Tony's eyes, Young Jeezy was the *realest* in the rap game.

Pretty Tony was halfway to the concert hall when he noticed a cop car following close behind him. He instinctively smashed the brake, crushed the burning cigarillo into the ashtray, and clicked his right blinker.

Wrong move. As soon as Pretty Tony made his turn, the officer flashed his lights.

Pretty Tony moved quickly to access the stash box inside the dash. He quickly tapped a series of buttons on the GPS system, pressed in on the lighter component, and out whizzed a two-and-a-half-inch-thick titanium box from behind the radio unit.

Pretty peeled the snub-nose .44 Bulldog revolver from his waistline—and the ounce of odorous reefer from his pant pocket—and shoved them both into the stash box. He sprayed a few squirts of Citrus Blast air freshener into the vent, flattened his t-shirt and waited for the white patrol cop to approach his window.

$$$

Officer Tom Sheller—a cop of twenty two years—despised guys like Anthony Johnston. He hated drug dealers, the way they dressed, the way they talked, and most definitely, the flashy vehicles they drove. They were all assholes—assholes who deserved to be in prison. With his right hand clutched on his service weapon, left hand wrapped around his flashlight, Sheller knocked twice on the darkly tinted window.

When the driver of the BMW rolled down his window, a thick cloud of orangish-blue smoke billowed out toward the dark sky. Sheller immediately took note of the driver's bloodshot eyes and the huge diamond-studded necklace that hung proudly around his scrawny brown neck.

Damn thing must've cost a fortune, Sheller thought. *I knew he was a dealer. I friggin knew it!*

Sheller squeezed the handle of his holstered weapon a tad tighter. "License 'n' registration?" he asked, all the while scanning the inside of the vehicle.

"How's it going, officer?"

"License 'n' registration."

"It's in my glove compartment," replied the driver. "You mind tellin' me why you pulled me over?"

"Speeding," spat Sheller. "You were doin' seventy-two in a thirty-mile-an-hour zone."

The driver glanced at his dashboard. "Seventy-two? Shit. I didn't notice I was goin' that fast."

"Hmp. Sure you didn't. Probably all the marijuana you been smoking."

The driver flashed a nervous smile. "Naw. I don't think that's the case, officer. I only had a couple of puffs."

"Sure you did. Any more dope in the car?"

"N-naw," he responded quickly. "Absolutely not. That's all I had, sir."

"And you're sure? Wouldn't happen to be lying would you? You are aware that it's a criminal offense to lie to a cop, right? Obstruction of official police business is what it's called."

"I ain't lying, sir. Ain't no more dope in the car."

The driver of the BMW was obviously nervous.

"Hm. How about weapons? Any of those in there?"

The driver shook his head. "No, no sir. No drugs or weapons. None."

Sheller suddenly yanked the driver side door open. "Step out of the car. Now!" he blasted

"Why? What'd I do, officer? I got all of my paperwork."

"I said step out of the car, boy!"

When the driver of the BMW dismally exited the vehicle, Sheller immediately snatched him up by his belt loops. "Hands on the hood! Now! I said on the hood! Good. Good. Now spread your legs… Spread 'em! Further. Further. Atta boy… Now, see how easy that was?"

Sheller bent the driver's arms back and slapped a pair of shiny silver handcuffs on his wrist.

"What's this about, officer?"

"You're a drug dealer, that's what it's about. You're going down!"

"A drug dealer? Goin' down? I ain't no…"

Sheller reached into the driver's pant pocket and pulled out a gigantic wad of cash. "Then what's this? Mind tellin' me how you got all this cash?"

"I um… I'm a uhh… A used car salesman."

Sheller smiled. "Good one. Never heard of that before."

"It's true, officer. You can check me out if you want. I work at…"

"Never mind that. I'll settle with you telling me how much cash this is. Can you do that?"

"I uh… I think it's 'bout, umm… About, umm…"

"And you mean to tell me you don't even know how much money you're toting around?"

"Well, I uh, no. See… I um… I made two sales today, a Buick Park Avenue and a…."

"Save it, son. I'm gonna conduct a search on your vehicle. Anything you wanna tell me? Make it easy on yourself now?"

"I'm not a bad dude, officer. I smoke a lil' weed, sell a few used cars, that's it. If you don't mind you can jus' write me a ticket 'n' let me go."

"Not gonna happen. Not today anyhow. What I'm gonna do is place you in custody while I search your vehicle. If you're telling the truth, about not having anything in there, then you'll be on your way in no time. If not—if you do have something illegal in there—and I will find it—then it's County Lockup for you buddy, no breaks. Now, right this way." Sheller stuffed Johnston into the backseat of his cruiser and took off back towards the BMW.

Three times Sheller searched the interior and exterior of the BMW, and each time he came up with the same thing: nothing. *Well, aside from the pungent marijuana roach in the ashtray. But, what was that? A friggin fifty-five dollar citation? Hell no.* Sheller knew there was something of greater value inside that vehicle; he just hadn't found it yet!

Sheller looked over his shoulder at the detainee, then down at the marijuana partial in the ashtray and back over his shoulder, again.

Sheller pressed in on the side of his walkie-talkie and spoke into its base. "Forty-two to dispatch," he said. "Forty-two to dispatch… Officer requesting K-9 Unit on Main and Monument… I repeat, Officer requesting K-9 Unit on the corner of Main and Monument."

"Copy that forty-two. K-9 Unit is in route."

Approximately seventeen minutes after radioing in to dispatch, Officer Skid, a pot-bellied older Caucasian man with a deteriorating comb over and a thick mustache, pulled up to the curb in a K-9 unit. He exited the vehicle, hobbled over towards the BMW and waved. "How's it goin', Sheller?"

"Fine," replied Sheller.

"Except for?"

"Except for we got this here ass-bag hiding something in his vehicle."

"And?" asked Skid, clearly being facetious.

"And, and I can't find it."

Skid chuckled. "Well, how do you know he's got somethin' in his vehicle, Sheller, if you can't find it?"

Sheller's face flushed and he gritted his teeth. "Because, I can feel it, Skid! That's how!"

"Because you can feel it, huh?"

"Sure. The man had close to fourteen thousand in his pocket."

"So?"

"Fourteen thousand, Skid. Fourteen thousand, in cash."

"Did you ask how he got it?"

"Sure did. Fucking punk lied and said he sold used cars for a living."

Skid shook his head. "So, lemme guess, you want me to have Jerome sniff around, huh?"

"Why else would I summon a K-9, Skid?"

Skid looked back at the detainee. "You wouldn't be asking me to conduct an illegal search, would you?"

"An illegal search? Fuck, Skid! That goddamn nigger back there blew marijuana smoke in my face like it was legal. Is that enough to warrant a fucking search?"

"Now calm down, Sheller," said Skid, his hands out before his chest. "There isn't any need for swearing. I get your point, good and clear. I'll send Jerome over, and rest assured, if there's anything in his vehicle to be found, Jerome will find it."

Sheller faked a smile. "Great."

Like always, Skid followed protocol by jotting down the time of incident, the name of the officer involved in the traffic stop, as well as the perpetrator's registration number. Then he released Jerome.

In a flash Jerome was out of the cruiser sniffing around the BMW: the engine compartment, tire wells, the trunk compartment, and of course, the vehicle's interior. Jerome searched the entire vehicle and came up with nothing. Well, nothing aside from the marijuana roach.

Skid leaned into the vehicle and retrieved the roach. "Looks to me like this is all your boy has, Sheller."

"I'm not buyin' it," held Sheller, "Have the dog check once more. I know he's dirty, Skid."

"Now, Sheller, we can't be spending all night out here. There's real criminals out there you know."

"Real criminals? C'mon now, Skid. I have a strong feeling about this one. Have him check it one more time. Just one more time. I'm begging you, for God's sake."

Skid took a deep breath and rubbed his mustache. "All right, Sheller. But you're paying for drinks at the tavern tonight. Deal?"

"No problem, Skid. As many as you want."

And that was that. Skid sent Jerome back to search the vehicle, again.

As he did the first time, Jerome searched the engine compartment, tire wells, the trunk compartment, and of course, the vehicle's interior. And just like before, he only showed interest in the marijuana roach in the ashtray. Jerome pawed at it.

"Well, Sheller…" Skid said pointing at the dog, "My partner say's there isn't anything illegal in there aside from marijuana partial in the ashtray. Can you live with that?"

"You sure his sniffer ain't broken."

Skid laughed. "Good try, Sheller. But Jerome is one of the best of his kind. If there was something inside of that vehicle—other than the marijuana of course—you'd hear Jerome barking like a mad prairie dog. He'd be howling at the moon right now."

Suddenly, Jerome barked.

"Roof! Roof! Roof, roof, roof!" he exclaimed and began violently scratching at the dashboard.

Skid looked over at Sheller with a pair of raised eyebrows. "Well I'll be dammed. Guess there is something in there."

"I knew it!" jumped Sheller. "Let's tear it apart!"

Sheller and Skid took to destroying the vehicle immediately. With crowbars and flathead screwdrivers, they pried into every nook and cranny of the BMW's interior, even going so far as to cut holes in the genuine leather seats and dash. But they were getting nowhere. This wasn't another piece of junk they were dealing with. This was foreign craftsmanship at its best.

"It's gonna take some heavy tools to crack this one, huh, Skid?"

"Um-hm. Crowbars aren't gonna get it."

"What you say? Take it to the station, and let Ned rip it apart?"

"Guess we don't have a choice, huh?" said Skid. "Unless, wait! Maybe it's a lockbox."

"A what-box?" questioned Sheller.

"A lockbox. Or, some people call them stash boxes."

"What are they?"

"Move over," said Skid. He planted his fat ass in the driver seat of the BMW and began randomly pressing on the dash. "I've seen these things before. Usually they're made of titanium or steel."

"How do they work?"

"They're controlled by a specific array of buttons, and when entered in sequence, a digital signal is sent to the box commanding it to open. It's all state of the art. Only the big time dealers have them."

Sheller was intrigued. "And you say they're made of titanium, huh?"

"Sure. Either that or steel."

"And that'll explain why the dog didn't smell it at first, huh?"

"Sure will."

"Hm. And how do we get the code?"

Skid looked back at the detainee. "Guess you have to ask someone who knows."

Sheller stormed off towards the cruiser in a fit of rage. He snatched open the back door, grabbed the detainee by his collar, and yelled "What's the friggin code?" in his face.

"Code? Man, I don't—oomph! Oh, shit! Ah! Ahh! Ahhhhh!" he yelled as Sheller punched him in the temple repeatedly. "Oh, shit! Come on man. Ahhhh!"

"Don't fuck with me! Give me the code! Give me the goddamn code!"

"I told you I ain't—ahhh! Ahhh! Come on, man… Ahhhhhh!"

Skid intervened with a sharp whistle. "Hey, Shell! I got it! I cracked the code! We got more dope and a firearm over here, bud!"

$$$

Pretty Tony was balled up in the corner of the cop car bleeding from his head when Skid popped the code. He could do nothing but sit back and watch as he got caught up in the snowball that officially ruined his life.

After evidence was bagged and tagged, and the tow truck arrived, Pretty Tony was taken to County Lockup. He was booked on six felony charges, and if found guilty, he'd face up to ten years in prison (a minimum of five with a plea agreement).

But, at that point, that was the least of his worries. The Feds had much more in store for him.

After being searched, fingerprinted and fed Pretty Tony was offered his free phone call.

"And the number you wish to call?" the blue-eyed, blonde-haired bailiff asked.

"481," he said with much haste, "4155. Clive Daniels. Attorney Clive Daniels."

Four rings into the call a groggy-voiced and sleep-deprived Clive Daniels answered the telephone. "He—hello?"

"Clive, its Anthony Johnston. I'm in County Lockup."

Mr. Daniels cleared his throat. "Jeez, what time is it?"

"Three a.m. I need you to get me out of here."

"Three a.m.? How long you been there?"

"Too long."

"What for?"

"Some racist-ass cop pulled me over and found my…"

Mr. Daniels instinctively intervened. "Not another word, Mr. Johnston. I'll—I'll be there in an hour. I have a friend who's a bail bondsman. Let me see what they have on you and I'll post bail. Just be patient. I'll be there after awhile."

Pretty Tony smiled. "Smooth. I'm waiting, Clive."

Mr. Daniels rose and rubbed his eyes. "No problem," he said. "Just remember, don't say a word, Mr. Johnston. To anybody."

"Ye—yeah," he said nodding, "I already know the script. It's done. Just come get me, Clive. I got shit to handle."

Pretty Tony took a seat in one of many hard plastic chairs and waited for his attorney to bail him out. Twenty-eight minutes into his wait, a busty brown-skinned bailiff with hazel eyes and bob hairstyle called his name.

"Mr. Johnston?" she said looking down at her clipboard. "Mr. Anthony Johnston?"

Pretty Tony stood to his feet and smiled. "That's me. Anthony Johnston, that's me."

"Wonderful. Right this way, please," she said with a bright white smile. The bailiff led Pretty Tony around a corner and down a long hallway with a series of doors on either side. She stopped when she came to a thick steel door bearing a plaque with the words **Interrogation Room 6** on it. The bailiff knocked twice and waited for a response.

Pretty Tony swallowed nervously, his brow furrowed with confusion. "Excuse me, miss, but do you mind tellin' me what we doin' here?"

The bailiff knocked twice more and looked down at her clipboard. "Federal Agent Ted Steele wants to see you."

"Federal Agent?" Pretty Tony said with a step backwards. "Hell naw, I posted bail. My attorney is Clive Daniels. I just spoke to 'im."

"I'm sorry, Mr. Johnston," said the bailiff with another swift knock on the door, "but that's not my problem. I'm just the transporting bailiff. They send and I deliver."

"But my lawyer told me…"

In the middle of his sentence, a man of maybe forty-two years approached. He stood at five foot eight, weighed nearly one hundred and seventy pounds, and wore his hair low and faded. A gold badge hung from his neck that read Agent.

"There you two are," he said with a steaming cup of coffee in his right hand, Manila folder in the left. "I thought I'd miss you… How's life been treating you, Ms. Moore?"

The bailiff flashed a beckoning smile. "Oh, I've been okay. And you?"

"I'm here," he said as he opened the interrogation room door. "I see you tracked down Mr. Johnston, hey?"

Miss Moore looked down at her clipboard. "One Mr. Anthony Johnston, just like you ordered."

Agent Steele flashed a refreshing smile. "Thanks, lovely. You're a dear."

She blushed. "No problem. Just give me a ring when you're done."

"Will do."

Agent Steele ushered Pretty Tony into the interrogation room and motioned for him to sit at the wooden table before them. "Mr. Johnston," he began, wasting no time. "I know you're probably wondering why you're here, right? Well, I have a few questions to ask you. If you answer them you can be on your merry way."

"And if I don't?"

"If you don't, then, we'll have ourselves a problem won't we?"

"I guess so."

Agent Steele took a sip of his coffee. "There's no need for problems, right, Mr. Johnston?"

"Shit, I don't know. You tell me. You're the one asking questions."
Agent Steele took another sip of his coffee. "Mr. Johnston, I only wanna know who killed…"
"I refuse," Pretty Tony said in a rather causal manner.
Agent Steele chuckled. "You refuse? Ha. You refuse?"
"Yeah. You heard me, I refuse. I wanna go back to lockup."
"And just who do you think I am, Mr. Johnston? A patrolman? A State employee? Did you or did you not see the badge? Can't you read? It says Federal Bureau of Investigation, in case you can't. You're not in the little leagues anymore buddy."
 "I don't care who you are, or who you work for. I ain't no rat, and that's that. I don't associate with cops, and I don't know shit about nothing, plain and simple. Now, if you don't mind, I'd like to go back to lockup. My attorney's posting my bail."
"Who? Clive Daniels?" Agent Steele said with a smile. "Don't look so surprised, Mr. Johnston. Agent Steele knows everything… I know where you operate, how you operate, and who you operate with… I know your primary residence is a lavish loft located downtown on Wilshire Boulevard, and that your secondary source of habitation is a duplex residence just off Temple Drive… You drive a black BMW 745i, Ohio license plate number BTI-8135, registered to one Ms. Denise Johnston, who happens to be your ailing mother. I'm aware that you fly back and forth from Ohio to California once a month—to, I assume, meet with your California connection—and that you spend exactly two days on the trip each time you make it. You have two main women with whom you alternate regularly, one of which is expecting a child next month—a boy. You brought a Presidential Rolex watch from Kay's Jeweler last month on the 12th, and you have your vehicle detailed at a place called Jay's Custom Wheels on Gettysburg. Your cell phone number is 206-4400, and you're very found of Chinese food. Does that prove my point, Mr. Johnston?"
"What the fuck do you want from me?"
"A colleague of mine was killed two weeks ago. I need to know why and by whom."
"I don't know nothing about anybody getting killed."
"I didn't say *anybody*, Mr. Johnston, I said my colleague. He was also my friend, you know."
"Didn't know that. Sorry for your loss. But, like I said, I don't know anything about him getting killed."
Agent Steele smirked. "Mr. Johnston did I or did I not just prove to you who you are?"
"I mean, you told me a few things about myself… but still, I don't know shit 'bout no dead fed."

"So you wanna play hardball, hey? Well, tell me this, Mr. Johnston… do you know the three informants I sent at you last month?"

"Three informants?"

"Sure. The three informants each to whom you sold a kilo of cocaine to."

"A ki'?" he asked with a nervous smile. "You bluffin'. I don't even sell coke, I sell weed."

"Hm. Sure about that, Mr. Johnston?"

"Positive."

Agent Steele reached inside the Manila envelope and pulled out several 8x10 photographs of Pretty Tony meeting with various individuals.

"Remember now, Mr. Johnston? I told you I knew everything, didn't I? Now, do you wanna help me?"

Pretty Tony held his breath while he flipped through the photographs. "And what if I can't help you?" he asked, never once taking his eyes off the photos.

"Then I'll make you're life a living hell," Agent Steele said forthrightly. "I'll make you wish you'd have helped me, Mr. Johnston. I'll go down the line and charge everybody you love with federal drug trafficking and money laundering charges. Your mother, your kid's mothers, everyone! Your kids'll be thrown in foster care, and I'll make sure that everybody in Big Sandy thinks you're a rat. You're mother will die in a cold, lonely jail cell, and if the appeals court is lenient, your children's mothers will be out by the time their children have children. Now, is this the life you want for yourself and your family, Mr. Johnston?"

No, this is obviously not what Pretty Tony wanted. He was in absolute ruin. But he still had a decision to make. Either he'd remain loyal to the streets, by honoring the Code of Omerta, or he'd save his mother and children the heartache and anguish of imprisonment?

"What you wanna know?" he asked with tears forming in his eyes.

"Everything," replied Agent Steele.

Pretty Tony inhaled deeply. "Everything?"

"Everything."

"And you'll drop all charges against me and my family?"

"Sure."

"All of 'em?"

"One hundred percent."

"But you have to tell me everything. No bullshit. I don't have time for games."

"I'll tell you everything you need to know, but can you put that on paper for me?"

Agent Steele smiled. "No problem."

Pretty Tony took a deep breath and adjusted himself in his seat, for he knew it'd be a long ride. "Okay. It all happened when…"

Chapter Two
Solution Turned Problem

Headlines for the Ohio Tribune read: **DRUG KINGPINS WITH OHIO TIES IN CUSTODY. AGENTS SEIZE MILLIONS IN CASH AND TONS OF DRUGS!**

"The Flenory brothers are miscreants, two of the largest drug dealers of our time. These guys were two true cocaine giants, masters of trafficking in illegal and illicit material—they managed to funnel tons of cocaine into our country on a monthly basis, and with manufacturing hubs in major states such as Texas, Georgia, Los Angeles, Florida, New York, and Ohio, these guys were only going to grow stronger and richer as the months progressed. Thanks to a vigilant task force, the Flenory brothers are behind bars for good. The streets of America can breathe again," said Agent Fidel Gillespie I a recent interview.

That was all hogwash! Their so-called 'solution' only created more of a problem in the end. The streets were in utter chaos after the takedown of Big Meech and Southwest T Flenory. Those dickheads created a countrywide drought when they disabled BMF. And sure, it may've seemed like a big accomplishment in the beginning. It always does. But I sure bet it didn't look the same when crime rose a whopping 210 percent did it?

The Flenory brothers were said to have spoken for over sixty percent of cocaine on the streets of America, and without them, a lot of people were forced to get paid by other means—by any means. Dealers turned into stickup men after the drought, and stickup men became brutal savages. People were getting robbed left and right, and quite naturally, bodies were dropping like flies.

The streets needed coke, and they needed coke badly.

Free Big Meech and Southwest T!

Chapter Three
Haters Gon' Hate

It had been only a month since the Flenory brothers were taken down and already the streets were suffering. Desmond "Dirty" Stephens was down bad. With only forty-two hundred in cash to his name and no valid source of income, the thirty-one-year-old narcotics dealer was beginning to panic. He desperately needed a new drug connection.

Something had to give. And it had to give, quickly.

$$$

Club 702, with its spacious grounds, modern architecture, and its expensive fixtures, was definitely the new *It*. People from all over the Midwest flocked to the lavish structure. The place was sleek, attractive, and trendy. Club 702 attracted a lot of big names—rappers, athletes, actors. It also attracted Tito Orvela, Dirty's soon-to-be Dominican cocaine connection.

Ohio was prime land for pretty much any hustler who wanted to get paid. There were a lot of opportunities in Ohio, and Tito wanted in on the action. He wanted to move up a notch on the social and economic bar. Tito considered his chances for claiming a slice of that action as he skillfully concealed forty-five kilos of uncut cocaine in his Hummer. As soon as he finished with the stash, he'd set his course for the Buckeye State.

For upwards of six months Tito Orvela bled the state of Ohio dry, and he did so by way of Dirty, a five-foot-five, one-hundred-and-thirty-pound runt so to speak. Tito delivered Dirty dozens of kilos each month, and like any drug dealer appreciative of his connection, Dirty relished in the luxury of having a nonstop current of blow at his disposal. Dirty made quite the name for himself. But like always, haters gon' hate.

$$$

From a small oval table located precisely twenty feet from the V.I.P., Nino and his partner K.T. watched Dirty with envious eyes. As with any other Thursday night in Club 702, Dirty and his crew were the epicenter of attention. Bottles of expensive champagne were popped left and right, pharmaceutical Ecstasy was passed out as if they were Tic Tacs, and high-grade marijuana burned as if it were legal. Yes, Dirty and his crew were exhibiting nightlife at its finest, but they were gaining the wrong attention in the process.

"Now you see why I hate bitch-niggas?" Nino asked K.T. Nino had dark skin and dark eyes and he bore a muscular physique attributable to his six stints in prison. He stood four inches shorter than his flunky of fourteen years, K.T., who stood at six foot five and weighed two hundred and eighty pounds, but Nino was still the leader of the two.

K.T. had practically been Nino's yes man every since the night they met at Don's crap house on Grand and Willard. The two have been inseparable ever since, with the exception of prison, of course.

K.T. nodded his head, agreeing with Nino. "Um-hm," he said being his usual idiotic self. "I'm feelin' you, dawg. Shit, that's why I hate bitch-niggas too, homie. They weak."

"You goddamn right they are!" said Nino with a pound of his fist against the weak club table. "Just look at that nigga. Who the fuck wear's a Mohawk? And that bitch think he stylin' too, don't he?"

"Yup. They say his name Dirty. Say he supplyin' the whole state blow."

"Is that right?"

"Yup. Heard he got a Mexican connect that give 'em ki's every week."

"Oh yeah?" Nino asked rubbing his palms together. "Well, uh, let's see if that nigga can take a lickin' and keep on tickin'. How you feel 'bout that?"

K.T. grinned goofily. "I'm wit it, Nino. Let's see if he still the man when that iron go clack-clack. Ha, ha!"

$$$

After the club let out, Dirty and five of his home-boys led a pack of high and horny women to a nearby hotel—where a lavish Presidential suite awaited them. Inside they partied like rock stars. More Ecstasy, champagne, and reefer were consumed, and by the morning's yawn the entire group had engaged in an orgy of nearly every perverse variation you could think of: one man, two women; One man, three women; One woman, two men; One woman, three men. By ten a.m., the only two people who remained were Toy and Dirty. They lay naked and sound asleep in the bed.

Toy was a twenty-seven-year-old belle, whom Dirty proved very fond of. He lusted for her body over and over again that night, and although he had the option of experiencing the flesh of several of her friends, between Toy's thick chocolate thighs was exactly where he had wanted to be. She had a firm breast, caramel-complexioned skin, and chinky almond eyes. Toy was beautiful.

When Dirty woke and noticed Toy lying beside him, fear set in. He knew better than to fall asleep around a woman like Toy. She was tainted, and he was worth too much money. Screwing her was one thing, but shacking up with her was another. Lucky for Dirty, Toy's ugly reputation didn't precede her.

Dirty's reason for panicking was Ramone, or Razor, as people call him in the streets. He was Toy's brother, and he was one sick motherfucker. He had a reputation for binding and torturing his victims before robbing and killing them. And the grotesque scar that traced the full length of his right cheek made him that much more nefarious. The stories he'd heard about

Razor terrified Dirty.

But Razor didn't jump out of the motel closet door and jump him like Dirty half expected him to. He never showed up at all. Dirty woke Toy up, got her dressed, and the two headed out across town to the west side.

With Toy sitting at leisure in the passenger seat of Dirty's charcoal-grey Porsche 911 Turbo, Dirty zoomed up South Euclid like a NASCAR racer. Dirty weaved in an out of traffic and parked cars on the narrow street until he reached 828 South Euclid. He smashed the brake, ushered Toy out of the car and peeled her off a few hundred dollars bills, and then zipped off down the block with just as much zeal as he'd zipped up.

Parched and low on gas, Dirty decided to make a quick stop at BP. He whipped the Porsche into the parking lot with the speed and agility of a grey wolf. But just as he did so, a battered four door Delta Eighty-Eight skidded to a halt in front of him. The Delta bore darkly tinted windows, chipped maroon paint, gunk covered hubcaps, and a primed left fender. It was a piece of shit.

Dirty smashed the brake to avoid slamming into the wreck, smoke filling the air as his tires screeched against the asphalt. He cursed and smacked the dash board before putting the Porsche into reverse.

But he wasn't going anywhere. Right behind him, nearly on his bumper, a black sedan boxed him in.

Dirty looked into the rearview mirror. "What the—?" he said, but before he could get out another syllable, the guy was all over him. He jumped out of the passenger side of the sedan, and scurried up to Dirty's driver side. He raised his pistol and swung.

$$$

Nino's first swing from the shattered Dirty's driver-side window, the second split his face open like a microwaved Ball Park frank. Blood gushed from the wound like a sliced water hose, while Dirty clutched his face and winced in pain. Nino was a pro at jobs like this.

He quickly shoved Dirty over into the passenger seat and skirted off wildly in the Porsche.

After fifteen minutes and a couple of hard blows later, all three vehicles pulled up in front of Dirty's Aunt Cynthia's house. And it was supposed to be a simple job. Get in, get out, and make sure to leave no witnesses. Nino's crew had pulled dozens of capers together; no one needed to be coached.

When they pulled up out front of the white-and-brown Victorian-style home, with its newly paved driveway and its expensive yard décor, Nino shoved his gun in Dirty's face.

"Who in dere?"

"No-no one," Dirty muttered in response. Blood poured out from the gash over his eye. He wiped and wiped at it with his T-shirt.

Nino smacked him in the left side of his head with the gun. "Don't fuck with me, nigga! I ain't come'ta play. Now who in the goddamn house?"

"Ah, shit! Nobody, man. I, I swear to God. My aunt, my aunt lives by herself. No one but her."

"And how you know the bitch ain't here?"

"'Cause her car ain't here, man."

"Well, where the fuck she at this time of day?"

"Probably grocery shoppin' or somethin, man. I don't know."

"Yeah, well, she better be. You got a key, nigga?"

"On my key ring. But listen… I..."

Nino smacked him in the head with the gun again. "You listen!" he blasted. "I'm runnin' dis fuckin' show. Now get out and take me to the money. Any funny shit and it'll be a bunch of slow singin' and flower bringin' for that aunt of yours. You feel me?"

Dirty didn't say another word. He complied.

Once inside the house, Dirty led the trio through the house. They crossed through the beige-carpeted living room, over the white-tiled kitchen floor, and down into the fully furnished basement where Dirty kept his stash.

Dirty trembled the entire time. The thought of his kidnappers getting rid of him after they got what they wanted plagued his mind.

When they reached the bottom of the basement stairs, Dirty stopped in his tracks.

"Fuck you waitin' on?" Nino yelled. "You think this shit a game, 'cause I'll show you this ain't no fuckin' game? You wanna die, nigga? Huh? Do you? I ain't think so. Now, get me my fuckin' money!"

The look in Nino eye's said he meant business.

Dirty led them to the rear of the basement and stopped near a sleek new washer and dryer unit. He glanced back at them. God only knew what was going through his head at the time. He shoved aside the dryer unit, removed a small throw rug, and revealed the face of his in-ground, fireproof safe.

After entering a code into the electronic keypad, the safe let off a mechanical hiss and it's door jarred open. Seconds later the basement reeked of cash.

As soon as the safe was open, Nino shoved Dirty aside and reached his black, ashy hands inside of it. When they emerged, they were filled with neatly bound bundles of crisp one-hundred-dollar bills. Dirty could do nothing but drop his head between his legs in shame. There were close to nine hundred thousand dollars in that safe.

"This what the fuck I'm talkin' 'bout!" Nino shouted and jumped in the air like a kid who'd just won a prize at a carnival game. "We on! We fuckin' on, niggas! Tie that nigga up K.T., and Slim, you toss me one of those pillow cases over there. It's time to get this cake."

But Just as Nino started to fill the pillow case, a door slammed upstairs. Then there were footsteps.

"Hold on," said Nino, with the bag of cash wrapped tightly around his right fist. He pointed the pistol at Dirty. "What the fuck was that? I said what the fuck was that?"

"I don't know," Dirty replied. "If you want I'll..."

"Sit the fuck down," Nino said in a loud whisper. "You ain't goin' nowhere. K.T., you cover the stairs. Slim, you find somethin' to tie this nigga up with. I got the cash. We'll shoot our way out if we have to."

$$$

Cynthia was putting away her groceries. Vanilla wafers went in the cabinet over the kitchen sink, milk in the fridge, and her canned goods were stored in the cabinet underneath the sink.

When she reached down to put away her canned goods, she noticed a trail of blood staining the kitchen floor. She squinted and observed it closely. It led completely through the living room and dining areas of the home and down into the basement, where her nephew Desmond stored some of his belongings.

Cynthia slowly eased the basement door open. "Desmond?" she called out, her voice slightly trembling. You down there, honey? If so, you need to say something. Auntie Cyn worried 'bout baby."

Silence prevailed. Cynthia knew something wasn't right. She took off towards her bedroom closet in a haste, maneuvering her short, plump body through the house with the speed and agility of a woman half her age. She removed a .32 automatic pistol from the black shoe box she kept it in and headed back downstairs.

The pistol was small and lightweight, but it helped her champion her fears. She didn't know who or what was in her home, bleeding everywhere, but she was sure about to find out. Cynthia removed the safety from the pistol and took the first step down into the basement. "Desmond, is that you, honey? Aunt Cyn on her way down. If you're down there, say something."

The wooden stairs gave a creak as she tiptoed down them, her shadow slowly creeping up the basement wall like a stalking ghoul. The gun trembled in her hand as she walked.

Five steps down the basement stairs, a startling sight caught Cynthia's eye. In the reflection of an old antique mirror her mother had given her before she died, Cynthia saw what appeared to be three figures standing in her basement. They were dressed in dark clothing, and one appeared to have a pistol in his hand. Cynthia didn't say another word. She raised her weapon and started shooting.

Full-metal jackets whizzed out from the .32 fast and hard, each one traveling their own course. The first bullet struck the washing machine, tearing through the piece of modern equipment like a razor blade through a paper sack. The second bullet from Cynthia's gun penetrated the old antique mirror her mother left her, shattering it into thousands of pieces. The third bullet tore straight through Nino's left arm, coming to rest in the concrete wall behind him; the fourth struck K.T. in the chest, nearly killing him on the spot. He let off three shots and collapsed to the basement floor.

$$$

The heat was officially on. Everything happened so quickly. Gun shots, grunts, his aunt on the basement floor screaming like a bloody banshee. It was mayhem. But it was life or death for Dirty, one of those situations where you either willingly hand your life over or you go out in a blaze.

In a blaze, then.

Nino was too focused on filling the pillowcase with Dirty's money to see Dirty coming at him. Dirty sprang from the ground and lunged at Nino with all his strength. He ran his shoulder blade into Nino's injured arm, and when Nino hit the ground, Dirty pounced on him like a mountain lion on an injured gazelle. Nino dropped the gun to the ground, and Dirty quickly snatched it. The rest was all bullets and gun smoke. Nino and his crew made off with five hundred grand that day.

This ain't over bitch, Dirty thought, over and over again. *This shit ain't over!*

Chapter Four
Back Inside Of Interrogation Room Six

Agent Steele snapped. "And what does that have to do with my agent's death, huh? Are you pulling my chain? Are you?' Because I'm telling you right now I'll fucking burn you. I'll be the bane of your existence, the bearer of bad news in every prison you visit. I'll fucking terrorize you, Johnston, and that's my word. Now tell me what I need to know. Now."

Pretty Tony adjusted himself in the chair. "Alright, dawg. Damn. Chill out. I'm just givin' you the details. You know, the fine print. I could sit here all day and tell you how your man's got killed, and even who killed 'im, but in the end you're still gonna wanna know *why* he got killed right? My point exactly. Now, if you don't mind, can I finish what I was sayin'? Good. So, after the robbery jumped off…"

Chapter Five
Payback's a Mutha…

It was approximately 4:22 a.m., the night after the robbery against Dirty, and Toy's cellular phone wouldn't stop ringing. The caller phoned her repetitively, demanding that she answer.

As her Motorola rested underneath a piece of loosely sprawled clothing, Toy rested underneath the naked body of a local hustler named Maceo, a tall and excessively slim brother with long cornroll braids and a pointed nose, reminding many people of the California rapper and actor Snoop Dog. But Maceo's street credibility far exceeded that of Snoop. Maceo was a true-to-life gangster. People in the streets respected him, some even feared him.

At least those who knew of his existence.

Toy hissed and rose to her feet. Had her phone been closer she would've simply shut it off and went back to sleep. But the distance between the two and the obvious persistence of the caller forced her to get up and answer it. Toy moved aside her lace bra and picked up the phone. "What!" she yelled into the receiver.

"Bitch you set me up!" the caller yelled back.

Toy wiped sleep from her eyes. "Set you up? Who the fuck is this?"

"Bitch this Dirty, you know who the fuck this is!"

"First off, *bitch*," Toy said with a soft sprint towards the hotel bathroom, in an effort not to wake her latest one night stand. "I got yo' bitch, right here, nigga. Now who the fuck are you and what the fuck do you want?"

"Bitch, I told you this Dirty. Why the fuck you do it?"

"Dirty? Dirty?" Toy said looking up at the ceiling, genuinely lost as to who the caller was. She had slept with more men in the past month than all three of the Kardashian sisters combined; there was no telling who the caller was.

"It's Dirty you, slut!"

"Dirty? I don't know no fuckin' Dirty."

"So you don't remember the niggas dick you was suckin' last night you funky-ass bitch!"

"Nigga, fuck you!" Toy yelled back.

"I'm tellin' you, Toy, those niggas shot my aunt, and they gon' pay. All you ma'fucka's gon' pay!"

"Wait, shot your aunt?" she said. "I don't know nothing about nobody getting shot. You don't think it was me do you?"

"Them bitch-ass niggas shot my aunt and clipped me for a half a mill, all you ma'fucka's gon' pay! All y'all!"

Things were getting serious. "Wait, wait, wait… I didn't have anything to do with..."

"Save it, bitch! Now either you tell me where those niggas at, right fuckin' now, or I'm killin' yo' whole fuckin' family! Where they at!"

Toy bent down and cupped the phone to her mouth with her hand. "Listen, Dirty... I swear on my daughter, I didn't have anything to do with it... Please... You have to believe me... My family is all I have... Please don't harm them."

"Look, I'ma tell you like this, those niggas got my cash, and they fucked my auntie up for life. Somebody gon' pay. Either it's gon' be you, or its gon' be them. You make the call."

Tears started falling from Toy's eyes. "But I... I... I swear... I didn't even..."

"I don't wanna hear that shit! Somebody gon' pay, and it's up to you to figure out who it's gon' be."

The only thing Toy could think of was to call her brother, Ramone. She hadn't spoken to him in weeks, which meant she damned sure didn't conspire with him to rob Dirty. But, if it was anyone she knew that had something to do with this mess, it'd be Ramone.

"Look," Toy managed to say between sniffles and the urge to sob, "just give me a few minutes. I'm gonna make a call and see if I can't find out something for you. Two minutes. Two minutes tops, okay?"

Dirty paused, momentarily. "Two minutes. That's all you got. Don't fuck with me, Toy. I'll kill all you ma'fucka's."

Click.

Toy clicked over and immediately phoned her brother. After what seemed to be an eternity, a groggy and half-sleeping Razor answered the phone. "Hello?"

"Ramone, please tell me you didn't do it again. Please."

"Toy, its damn near five o' clock in the morning, what the fuck are you talking about?"

"Just tell me you didn't do it again, Ramone. Please tell me you didn't."

"What are you talking about, Toy? Don't tell me Momma done called you again? I told that woman I was gonna come by and clean out that basement. Shit, she need'ta chill out."

"I ain't talking about Ma, Ramone. I'm talking about you robbing another one of my friends."

"Robbing another one of your friends? Well, first off, Toy, they're not your friends, they're your clientele. Secondly, it's too damn early to be calling with all this nonsense, and third of all, if I did or didn't rob one of those trickin'-ass niggas, it's my business, ain't it?"

"So you did? You did do it?"

"No, shit, Toy! I didn't rob any of those corny-ass lames you deal with. But if I did, it's my fuckin' business ain't it?"

"You made it my business when they called me talking about killing me, Ramone. But I bet you didn't even think that far into your little plan, did you?"

"They did what? Who dis nigga, Toy? Who is he? Text me dat nigga's resume right now. Don't nobody fuck with my people! Nobody!"

Toy dropped her head and buried it between her legs. She couldn't take it anymore. The streets were catching up to her.

$$$

By now, Maceo was out of the bed, up and at it. He heard Toy yelling at someone on the phone, and after what she'd just done to him in the bed, he felt compelled to rush to her aid.

Stark naked, clad only in his long braids and birthday suit, Maceo burst into the hotel bathroom. "What's goin' on, Toy? Who's that on the phone?" Maceo could hear the person on the opposite end of the phone shouting like a madman.

"Nobody. It's okay," Toy said.

"It's okay? No the fuck it ain't! Ain't no nigga 'bout'ta have my girl all upset, cryin' 'n' shit. Gimme the phone, Toy. Give it to me!" Maceo reached down and practically snatched the phone from Toy's hand. "Who dis?" he demanded to know. "I said who dis?"

"No, the question is who is this, and where is Toy?"

"Don't worry about Toy, nigga. She in reeeeal good hands."

"She in real good—nigga who the fuck is this?"

"Who is this?" Maceo shot back.

"This the nigga who's gone take yo' fuckin' life if you don't put Toy back on the phone, that's who this is."

"Take my life? You don't know me, dawg. This Maceo from Summit Courts, nigga. Ain't no bitches my way."

"Well, Mr. Maceo from Summit Courts, you 'bout'ta be Maceo from the morgue if you don't stop bullshitin' and put Toy back on the phone."

"Is that so?"

"You barkin' up the wrong tree, little nigga. Now put Toy back on the phone or call it quits."

Maceo scoffed. "You dead, nigga. Dead. Dead, you fuckin' hear me!" Click.

When Maceo ended the call, the guy on the other end was still shouting and yelling obscenities. Maceo dropped the phone at Toy's feet and got dressed.

The beef was officially on.

$$$

Both Dirty and Razor continuously called Toy's cell phone. But she didn't pick up for either of the two. She didn't know what to do. Toy didn't even answer Maceo when he inquired as to who the guy was on the phone. What had Razor started? Would this Dirty guy honor his threats against her and her family? What would she do if he actually harmed her mother and daughter, the only two positive things at that point life? Would she be able to survive on her own, or would she succumb to the ways of her past. She couldn't loose them. They were her crutch.

$$$

After one final call to Toy's cell phone, Dirty gave up. He tossed his phone on the passenger seat and reached into the glove compartment, removing a black ski mask, two P-89 Ruger handguns, a large bowie knife, and a pair of black leather gloves. Dirty had never done anything close to what he was about to do, but someone had to pay; they had to. And so, he slipped on the black leather gloves, cocked back both pistols, and shoved the knife in his waistline.

"Payback's a muthafucka!" he jumped the fence in the backyard of 828 South Euclid. "I'ma make 'em pay. I'ma make 'em all pay…"

Chapter Six
Death and Vengeance

Homicide detectives Dennis Farr and Elliot Polch arrived at 828 South Euclid Street at approximately 7:55 a.m. uniformed officers had already secured the scene—a sick and gruesome scene—and Farr had thus prepared himself for the sight.

Out of all his years on the force, Farr had never seen anything so hellish. Only a madman could create such a macabre spectacle. Streaks of crimson blood stained the carpet and the walls of the old rickety home, and the pungent smell of coagulating blood permeated the air so thickly that Farr could taste it in the back of his throat.

The place was a mess.

Farr, a tall and slender man of 47 years, with olive-toned skin, large hands, and sandy brown hair, reached down into the breast pocket of his cheap gray suit and pulled out a small hand-held device. He clicked the right side of the recorder, squatted down closely to the first victim's body, and spoke. "It's approximately 8:01 a.m., June 17th, and I'm here at the city's most recent homicide—a double homicide…"

Farr reached into his pant pocket and pulled out a spittle-covered handkerchief. "The first vic' is an African American female, who appears to be within the age span of late fifties, early sixties…" he said with the cloth to his mouth. "She appears to have suffered an apparent gunshot wound—close proximity—to the right side of her temporal lobe, which exited just above her left ocular ridge…"

Far took a deep breath and exhaled before finishing up his assessment of the first victim. "It seems as if vic' number one was trying to elude her attacker. The furniture and furnishings are in obvious disarray—lending credence to the fact that there was a struggle—and the manner in which we found the vic's clothing—torn and tattered—supports this theory."

Farr's knee's gave a loud and arthritic crunch when he rose. He looked over at one of the uniformed officers, Officer Ted Sanders, a recent transfer from the 8th Precinct, and asked, "And the other one?"

Officer Sanders pointed his long white finger towards the back of the home and added, "Follow me."

Nearly halfway down the excessively narrow hallway that stretched from the living room to the back rooms of the old, tired home, smothered with framed family photographs and plaques of various sorts and sizes, one of those pictures drew Farr's attention. It was the face of a criminal. The face of Ramone "Razor" Marshall.

The first thing that came to Farr's mind was karma. Yes, it was undoubtedly Razor's illicit and immoral actions that had led to the unfortunate events at

828 South Euclid. He had yet to finish assessing the scene, but Farr already knew the motive behind the crime: retaliation. He had been on Razor's tail for a long time now, trying to do his best to pin charges ranging from robbery, extortion, and murder on him, so he knew the feeling in his stomach was right before he even assessed the second victim.

Bloodshed will definitely follow, thought Farr. *There's no way he's gonna let this go.*

When Detective Farr entered the back bedroom, he saw Sanders standing beside a small, lifeless body. Multiple lacerations covered her tiny chocolate frame. She seemingly swam in a puddle of her own blood. The six-year-old had been attacked in her sleep, totally unbeknownst to the torment that lay ahead. Farr thought about his seven year old granddaughter upon first sight of the little girl.

Oh, he's definitely gonna paint the city red for this one… I just hope I can catch him before he does…

Chapter Seven
Razor, It's All Your Fault!

Everyone inside if McLin Funeral home was bereaved by the deaths of Mrs. Eartha Marshall and Baby Kia Spencer. Someone had maliciously murdered the woman and child, and neither of the two deserved it. Baby Kia did absolutely no wrong in her six years on earth, and the only mistake Mrs. Marshall made was giving birth to two hardheaded children: Ramone and Latoya.

Now, Toy was no angel—she was trouble to some degree—but she didn't come close to Ramone. He was Satanic, demonic even. Hell, his own family feared him at times. But he was their family at the end of the day, and that's all that mattered.

Dressed in a black hoodie, black jogging pants, and timberland boots, Razor approached his mother and his niece's caskets with tears in his eyes. How did he let this happen? How could he make such a huge mistake? Did he actually think he could escape the long hand of karma, or did he consider himself exempt to the laws and powers that be?

With tears streaming down his scarred face, jaw muscles bulging out the sides of his face like two throbbing fists, Razor stood overlooking Baby Kia's tiny casket with revenge in his heart. He'd surely torture and kill Maceo when he found him, and his entire family would follow.

Just as Razor turned to leave and walk off, Toy stepped up from the pew behind him. Razor opened his arms to give her a hug, but Toy reciprocated with an open-handed smack that set Razor's entire skull ablaze.

"You killed my baby!" she yelled. "You killed her! You killed my child, you bitch!"

Toy's harsh words and heavy blows increased in speed and strength. "I hate you, bitch! I hate you! You're the devil! I fucking hate you! Ahhhhh!"

Razor could do nothing but stand there and accept every blow that this grieving sister offered. After all, she was absolutely right. He was a piece of shit, and their blood stained his hands. But what was done was done. All he could do from that point on was to pay his enemies back with bloodshed of their own. He'd boil their children, sever the heads of the women, and castrate the men. People would remember Razor's evil deeds for generations to come. He'd be immortalized solely for his ability to inflict pain and death upon his enemies, in utterly remarkable ways.

Chapter Eight
Frienemies
(Hours after the robbery)

The bullet had pinged around inside of K.T. like a ping pong ball, first striking his lung, then his spleen, and ultimately his large intestine. As he lay with his head slumped over Crystals leg, his girlfriend of two and half years, he prayed for forgiveness.

God, forgive me of my sins… The sins I know I've committed, the sins I don't know I've committed, and the possible sins of my future… Dear God, please don't let me die like this… Please… Touch Nino's heart, Dear God… Make him change his mind… Give me one more chance, God. Just one… Just one more chance, God. Amen.

K.T. wanted Nino to break the rules, the rules he, Nino, and Slim had long agreed to. *No witnesses, no hospitals, and no talkin' to the cops if you're picked up.. We get in, get out, and never speak on the events again. Agreed?*

Agreed.

That was until K.T. needed medical attention. Now he wanted Nino to compromise. But Nino would never do such a thing, and K.T. knew it. For all they knew the woman was dead, and the cops were on their trail. Nino would never give in. K.T. was fucked.

$$\$\$\$$$

While Slim was out getting rid of the vehicle, Nino stood over the coffee table in Crystal's one bedroom apartment tallying up their take. Blood dripped from the bullet wound on his left arm, but Nino felt no pain. The cash was like morphine to him. At that time nothing else mattered, not K.T., not the old lady or her nephew, not even the cops. Nino had finally scored big. His days of scavenger hustling was over.

$$\$\$\$$$

For every bandage Crystal applied, K.T. lost another ounce of blood. The gaping wound in his chest wouldn't let up. He was dying before her very eyes. His face was flushed white, and his eyes were turning dark yellow. He wasn't going to make it much longer, and as it stood, Nino was his only chance of surviving.

K.T. looked over at Nino and uttered, "Hey, Nino, Dawg… I can't feel my legs… I can't… I can't…" then, suddenly, "Blooahhhh!" he spat up a mouthful of blood.

"Fuck that, Nino! I'm calling the ambulance!" she said. "I'm not about ta sit here and watch him die! I won't do it."

Just as Crystal turned and reached for the telephone, K.T. stopped her. With his last bit of energy, he reached out and grabbed her by the wrist. "No... no," he stammered. "Don't... Don't... Don't worry, Crys... Nin... Nino won't... He won't... He won't let me..." and then he heaved his last breath. "Urgghhhh." K.T.'s eyes rolled back into his head, his neck dropped over the edge of the couch, and he defecated himself.

K.T. was dead.

$$$

Nino watched as K.T.'s chest heaved up and down, and his eyes rolled back into his skull. Then the room reeked of feces. There was no doubt K.T. was dead. His time had come and gone.

Nino dropped the wad of cash he was counting and approached Crystal—a short, busty woman with caramel-complexioned skin, jade green eyes and black shoulder-length hair. He placed his hand on her shoulder. "It's gon' be a'ight, Ma'," he said assuringly. "It's gon' be a'ight."

"That's easy for you to say, Nino. But K.T. was all I had. He was my everything! And now he's gone," she yelled. "You killed him, Nino. You fucking killed him!" Crystal leaned down and hugged K.T's stiff body, sobbing uncontrolably.

Nino brushed Crystal's hair to the side and wiped a stream of tears from her face. "I know it hurts, but there was nothing I could do. K.T. knew the code."

Crystal rose to her feet. "The code? The code? Fuck you and your *comraderie* bullshit, Nino! Fuck you!" she blasted and smacked him in the face.

Nino shrugged it off and wrapped his arm around Crystal's tiny waist. He pulled her close and spoke into her ear. "I'm sorry, Crystal, but it is what it is. K.T. he knew the rules. Shit, we all did. And we all agreed not to break. That could've been me laying over there on that couch, and you know what? K.T. would've honored the code. He would've let me die like a gangster."

Crystal leaned back and looked into Nino's eyes. "A gangster? Is that how gangsters die, Nino, begging their friends to call for help? Is it?"

"That's just the way the cards fell, Crystal. Don't for one minute think he wasn't my mans, because he was."

"Just not enough to save his life, huh?"

"What more do you want me to say, Crystal? Shit went sour and K.T. lost his life. I'm saddened by all this shit, but at the end of the day life moves on."

Crystal had a blank expression on her face. "How can you be so heartless?"

"The streets."

Crystal dropped her head. "And what about me, Nino? What happens to me?"

Nino placed his hand on Crystal's chin and gently lifted her head. "I would never leave you fucked up, Crystal. Never. K.T. wouldn've never done it to my girl, and I won't do it to his."

"You say that now, but I'll probably never see you again after you walk out of that door."

"Never. I got you, baby. You're entirely too beautiful to be goin' without. Trust me, you'll never have to worry about money again." Nino placed his hand on the back of Crystal's neck and ran his finger from her shoulder line clear down her collarbone. Crystal flinched as Nino slid his hand down into her shirt.

"Mm. What are you doing, Nino?" she asked.

"Being here for you."

"And what's that suppose to mean?"

"It means I won't let you got without. You're with me now."

Crystal looked over at the mound of money on the table, then over to K.T. "Will you make sure he has a good funeral, Nino?"

"Of course I will. The best money can buy."

Neither said another word. Nino unzipped his pants, pulled out his penis and led Crystal down to her knees.

She sealed the deal with a kiss.

Literally.

Chapter Nine
Slippin'

Razor's digital wristwatch read 2:47 a.m. The night had been long and restless for him. It was coming up on the eighth hour into his stakeout. Still no sign of Maceo.

Maybe Bumble Bee lied… I should've never trusted that crack-head bitch.

Razor saw Bumble Bee earlier that day outside of a local beer and wine drive thru. She was up to her usual—loitering and soliciting outside of the establishment. She ran up aside Razor's vehicle as he eased his car out of the drive thru.

"Hey, baby," Bumble Bee said trotting alongside the car. "You want some of this?" she asked and raised her shirt, exposing her wrinkled A-cup breast. "It's ten for head, twenty for twat, and forty for backdoor action. Wha'cha say?"

Razor pressed the brake and shook his head. "I see a leopard never changes their spots, huh?"

Bumble Bee squinted. "Who's that… Ramone?" she asked, half-smiling. Razor met Bumble Bee when he was only thirteen years old. He had managed to maintain a off-again- on-again business relationship with her ever since. She taught him a great deal about the streets. She taught him how to con, steal, rob, and deal. Bumble Bee was the first woman to ever preform oral sex on Razor, as well as the only woman to ever pickpocket him. She was ancient on the dope scene, and, sadly, she hadn't changed one bit. Still scrawny and greatly unkempt, still auctioning off her flesh for cash.

"Is that you, Ramone? You look so different, boy. How long you been out?"

"Not long."

"Hm. You lookin' for a date? You know I ain't lost my touch." Bumble Bee stuck out her tounge and gave it a twirl.

Razor smiled. "Naw, I'm smooth on the date. But you can help finding somebody though."

"Who you lookin' for?"

"Just get in… Take a ride with me."

Within ten minutes, Razor had more on Dwight "Maceo" Gordon than the Bureau of Motor Vehicles. Turned out that Bumble Bee and Maceo's mother, Teresa, went to high school together, and pretty much remained friends throughout. On several occasions, Teresa took Bumble Bee along with her when she'd purchase drugs for the two of them from her son. Bumble Bee knew the address where Maceo lived, where he dealt, and possibly even where he kept his stash.

Maceo was fucked.

Razor gave Bumble Bee a hundred and fifty dollars in cash, dropped her off, and immediately headed to the address. It was time to find the guy who killed his mother and niece. Time for payback.

A lot of people went into and came out of the little white house on Seneca Lane, with it's paved driveway and Bermuda shutters, but no one fitting the description Bumble Bee gave him. The vehicle was sitting in the driveway—a white Navigator with white mag rims—but no sign of Maceo. Razor considered leaving and returning later, but just as he moved to start the car, Maceo staggered out from the residence with a seemingly underaged girl on his arm. She wore a tight-fitting dress, stiletto pumps, and gold bangles on her wrist.

Maceo chirpped his alarm and he and the girl jumped into the vehicle.

As soon as the Navigator's doors were closed, Razor flipped the safety on his Mac-11 sub-machine gun and grabbed the door handle. But before he jumped out to murder the two, a cop car pulled up.

"Fuck," Razor said and ducked down in his seat. "Just my luck."

The cruiser pulled up on the street behind Maceo's SUV, completely blocking his path. The tail end of the Navigator jerked as Maceo smashed on the brakes to avoid hitting the cop. Razor couldn't believe it. His luck was ridiculous. After eight whole hours of stalking, he was forced to watch another predator seize his prey.

But that wasn't the case. The officer never got out of his vehicle this day. In fact, he did nothing more than flashed his overhead lights and sound his siren before pulling off into the night. Razor was perplexed.

A warning? I can't believe this shit... Maybe...

Maceo backed out of the driveway, wildly, screeching his tires, fishtailing down the block. Razor started his vehicle and followed him.

Razor tailed Maceo, mimicking his movements as he whizzed in and out of the light-traffic-sprinkled streets, with little to no care as to who traveled the roads with him. Yes, Maceo was making the task quite difficult for Razor, but not impossible. Razor was a natural behind the wheel. At age ten hc was stealing his neighbor's cars for the pure pleasure of joy-riding, by twelve he was Reno's main larcenist, heisting between twenty and thirty high-end cars each week. Maceo would never get away from Razor. Never.

When Maceo pulled up outside of the Summit Courts Housing Projects, Razor let out a deep sigh of indignation. Summit Courts—a large row of red-brick buildings located on the city's Westside—was home to some of the most notorious killers and dealers in the city of Dayton, Ohio. There were dozens of unsolved murders there annually and hundreds of reports on drug dealing and prostitution. Even the cops were reluctant to respond there.

Razor had just pulled into a hornets nest.

Even in the wee hours of the morning, Summit Courts was teeming with life. *Hood rich* dope-boys stood outside of their candy-painted and kitted-up cars, laughing and joking with other locals, while scantily-clad women paraded around the red-brick labyrinth, in lure of their new baby-daddy, or at worse, a generous-trick willing and ready to compensate them for their ability to perform in the bedroom.

Razor sat back and watched as Maceo and the girl exited the Navigator, parted the sea of locals, and entered Building No. 6. He leaned back in his seat, lit a cigarette, and waited on his mark to return.

About half an hour later, Maceo emerged alone. He jumped back into his SUV and skirted out of the parking lot. Razor followed.

Maceo stopped in front of a two-story, four-unit apartment building just off of Riverview Ave.

Razor silenced his engine, and waited for Maceo to exit the vehicle

Maceo got out and entered the apartment building, and right behind him was Razor, sprinting across the quiet street towards the building with a flash light in one hand, sub-machine gun in the other. He approached the apartment complex in stealth, his burly frame swift and agile like a black leopard.

Two of the four units were lit up like a broadway opening, the other two showed no signs of vitality. That is, until Maceo entered his apartment—apartment 2. From then on his movements were as simple as a childish game to Razor: connect the dots or follow the leader, so to speak. Instead of approaching the front door, Razor took to the right side of the building and peeked inside the window at Maceo. Razor watched as Maceo maneuvered his tall, slender frame through the lavish apartment—his long braids swinging back and forth as he walked—and couldn't help but think how easy it'd be to kill Maceo right then and there. But Razor couldn't do it like that. He wanted—no he needed—to look Maceo in the eyes before he killed him. He wanted Maceo to beg for his life right before he took it. When Maceo entered his bedroom and started to undress, Razor doubled back and took to the main door of the apartment building. He walked to the door of apartment 2, raised his size twelve Timberland construction boot, and smashed it against Maceo's front door.

"Police! Police!" Razor yelled and ran into the apartment. "Search warrant! Come out of the room with your hands up!"

Razor heard shuffling in the back room. He contemplated on shooting the place up, but before he was forced to do such a thing, Maceo emerged from the bedroom with his hands in the air.

"Okay, okay," he said walking into the front room of the apartment, "don't shoot. I'm comin' out, don't shoot!"

Maceo turned the corner and met the barrel of the Mac-11.

"Stop right there," Razor commanded. "Don't move… Slowly—I said slowly!—now, get on your knees. That's right, down. And put your hands behind your head. Do it!"

Maceo complied. He moved slowly to his knees, fingers interlocked behind his head.

"Wait, you're not a co..." said Maceo and started to his feet.

Razor pulled the hair-pin trigger. Five bullets spat out from his barrel, two striking Maceo in the left forearm, one in the wrist, and another just below his left collarbone.

Maceo fell back to his knees and yelled out in agony, blood squirting from his arm and chest in torrents. "Ahh! Ahhhhhhh!" he screamed. "Please. Don't..." but before he could get out another word, Razor aimed the gun at his legs and pulled the trigger. Four more struck Maceo in his lower extremities: three tore through his left leg, the other through his right.

Maceo howled in pain. The sound echoed throughout the entire complex, undoubtedly awaking those snoozing tenants. But it didn't last long, for Razor cocked back his arm and swung the weapon at Maceo's face.

The first blow caused Maceo to bite his tongue in half, the second claimed his two front teeth. They flew across the room and bounced about the wooden floor like a set of ivory dice. Razor then straddled Maceo, beating him savagely with the weapon. "You killed my Momma! You killed them!" Razor yelled just before he shoved the barrel of the Mac-11 underneath Maceo's chin. "You killed them…"

Razor was about to pull the trigger and ended Maceo's life when someone shouted from the hallway.

"Police, everybody okay in here?"

$$$

At 6:20 a.m. dispatch received a call of shots fired at 222 West Senegal Street. Within four minutes of that call Veteran Officer Tom Shellar and three of his buddies from Precinct 5 were in route. Exactly two and a half minutes afterward, they were on scene.

"Jones and Parks you take the left," ordered Shellar, "O'Malley, you follow me."

When Shellar approached the splintered door of Apartment No. 2, the smell of fresh gunpowder soot poured out. He quickly peeked his head inside. "I'm going in… Cover me!"

Sheller dipped into the doorway with his weapon in front of him. "Police," he called out in his most authoritative voice, "everybody okay in here?" The only response given were about 8-10 shots from what sounded to be an automatic weapon. Shellar let off two shots, dove for cover and radioed for backup. The accompanying officers rushed to the scene as quickly as possible, but it was too late. One guy was dead, and the apparent assailant had escaped.

Chapter Ten

The Truth Amidst Lies

Three theories had circulated regarding Maceo's death—all of them plausible to some extent, but only one of them was true.

The first theory revolves around Maceo and MS-13, a savage Latino street gang widely known for its ties in illegal drugs, arms, and human-trafficking, stemming from El Salvador, Mexico. Word around town was that Maceo found one of their stash houses, cleared it out, and as a result had a hundred-thousand-dollar hit placed on his head; which, someone carried out.

Theory number two involves a woman named Toy. It was said that Toy conspired with her older brother, Razor, to rob and kill Maceo.

The final theory is a combination of both theory number one and two. It suggests that Maceo had in fact been shot by Toy's older brother Razor, but that he was alive when a group of no-good, dirty cops stormed in Maceo's apartment and stumbled up on twenty-two kilos of uncut coke that Maceo had stolen from MS-13. The cops killed Maceo, took the drugs, and redistributed the marked kilos back onto the streets of Dayton, Ohio. But truth is rarely as simple as that…

$$$

Twenty-nine-year-old Karen Gilbert, of Apartment No. 3, 222 West Senegal Street, was Maceo's neighbor, lover, and prime witness to his murder. Karen, present at the time of the incident, could verify that Maceo was in fact alive when the first group of uniformed officers arrived, and that it was one of them that killed him.

Karen was awakened by gunfire. The clamoring was so loud and piercing that it almost sounded as if the shooter were in the room with her. Karen dove for cover in the corner of her bedroom. After the second set of gunshots, she mustered up enough courage to grab the portable phone from her nightstand and phone the cops.

After the first group of cops arrived, Karen heard the third set of gunshots. They were different from the first two sets of gunshots—which were "machine-gun" like in style. They weren't as loud as the first two sets of gunshots, nor were they as close in sequence. Karen figured the second to be a handgun. Moments later there was shouting below—who she believes were cops—and a pair of headlights emerged in the grass out back. When Karen peeked out of her back window she observed several uniformed cops standing out back by a marked squad car. Just after, a tall,

Caucasion officer emerged with two black bags in his hands and loaded them into the trunk of the cruiser. Moments later the entire complex was surrounded with EMT's and additional police personnel.

Karen was questioned as to the events that had transpired that night—needless to say by the very officers implicated in Maceo's murder—but she swore that she had been sound asleep during the entire incident.

"And you mean to tell me you heard nothing?" asked Officer Tom Sheller of Precinct 5.

"No, sir," Karen answered with a straight face. "Nothing. All I know was I'm lying in bed asleep and then I hear you banging on my door."

"So I take it you don't wish to give a statement?"

"I don't know anything, sir. If I did I most certainly would."

"Well, if anything changes—if you happen to remember anything—feel free to give me a call," said the officer. He handed Karen one of his business cards and left.

Karen vowed never to tell anyone what happened that night. She was fearful of Maceo's killers returning and killing her for the secrets they shared. But, the burden was weighing too heavily on her. She had to tell someone what happened. Only problem was, she told the wrong person…

$$$

Big Jay hadn't taken the news well. He and Maceo were best friends. They were like brothers, thick as thieves. They did practically everything together. They were one another's shadow. Women and death were the only two things that ever separated the two.

It was two weeks after Maceo's death that Big Jay first heard of the third theory. It happened by sheer chance, too. Big Jay just so happened to know someone, who knew someone, who in turn, knew of a chick that knew Ronda, Karen's best friend. Ronda told her what Karen told her, and the story just traveled. It took two weeks to reach Big Jay, and another two weeks for Big Jay to find Karen to confirm the validity of the story. He finally ran into her at a local 7-11.

When Big Jay noticed Karen, she was busily blabbing off to her friend Ronda near the potato chip aisle. Big Jay immediately approached her.

"What's up, Karen?" asked Big Jay, as he stood closely in front of her, shifting his weight, hovering well above her head, making it nearly impossible to look him in the eyes.

Karen's face dropped. "H-hey, Jay. Lo-long time."

"Why you been avoidin' me, Karen? Why you actin' all guilty and shit?"

"Guilty? I ain't—I just been staying with my friend, Ronda. You remember Ronda don't you, Jay?"

For a second, Big Jay cut his eyes over at Ronda, who stood attentive with her hand shoved down into her Gucci purse, but his attention soon turned back to Karen. "You ain't been home in two weeks. What's the deal with that?"

"I… I… Thing's just aren't the same, you know?" Karen said in a cracked voice.

"I know; I know exactly how you feel."

"They killed him, Jay. They fucking killed him." Tears began falling down Karen's face. Big Jay reached out and smeared them into her smooth, brown cheeks.

"Karen, listen to me… I need to know exactly what happened that night, and I need to know now. Is there somewhere we can go and talk; my crib, or Ronda's maybe?"

Karen looked over at Ronda with questioning eyes.

"Its cool, girl" said Ronda. "We can go to my place. You guy's can talk there…"

$$$

Big Jay stood with his back against the apartment door enraged and teary-eyed as Karen delivered him the bad news. "I'ma get 'em back, Karen. I swear. Each and every one of those muthafuckas!"

"Just don't go doing anything irrational."

"Fuck that!" he shouted. "Those muthafucka's gotta die, all of 'em!"

"I understand, Jay, I do. And I agree. But, don't let your emotions get the best of you. Calm down and think before you act."

"You know what," Jay said wiping his face and adjusting his composure, "you're right, Karen. That ain't gon' get me nowhere but dead or in jail. Proper preparation prevents poor preformance."

Karen smiled. "Now that's the Big Jay I know. Don't be lettin' your emotions get the best of you boy."

Big Jay smiled. "You're right. You' re absolutely right, Karen."

"I know. Now here, take this," she said, handing Big Jay the business card Officer Sheller had given her. "That cop gave it to me, told me to call him if I remembered anything. I'm pretty sure it'll help out."

Big Jay looked down at the card. "Thanks Karen. I appricate this dearly. I do."

"No problem. Just be careful and keep in contact, okay?"

"No doubt."

Karen and Jay hugged. He kissed her on the forehead, and then he left.

That was the last Karen ever saw of him.

Chapter Eleven
Queen of the City

Although Dirty had never murdered anyone before, he knew very well what had to be done. He needed to make a statement—a bold one. One that said he wasn't a lame. Then no one would test him. If he didn't strike back, he ran the risk of never making money in Ohio again. Dirty handled his business.

After taking care of the old lady and the little girl, Dirty packed his things and headed east, to D.C. Best to shack up with Queeny.

Dirty and Queeny had done business together quite a few times in the past, during which she'd always advise him to stay a while. But Dirty had never been a fan of playing on another man's (or in this case, woman's) turf; he favored the home court advantage. But, now things were terribly different. He needed a place to lay low, and D.C. was the first place that came to mind.

Queeny was a firecracker. Her native roots were Haitian-Jamaican, but she'd been in the states so long that she'd been pretty much Americanized. She spoke and dressed like an American, but her stern disposition and short temper exposed her roots. Queeny was a hothead, one that, by her own admission, would *kill, torture, and torment* any person in her way. Queeny had been named and nabbed on countless murders in D.C., all of which she beat due to insufficient evidence.

Queeny's physical description didn't coincide with her reputation. One would expect a person of such nefarious talk to look somewhat unsightly, but Queeny was the farthest thing from ugly that Dirty knew of.

With light-brown skin, icy-white teeth, cat-like eyes and shoulder-length dreadlocks, Queeny was definitely a striking woman. Even underneath all the baggy men's attire, Dirty could tell Queeny had a body out of this world. The body of a belly dancer came to mind, or, better yet, a West Indes Calypso dancer. Dirty imagined a smooth, flat stomach on Queeny—possibly pierced—with a pair of nice, tight tits, a heart-shaped ass, a shaved vagina, and maybe even a tattoo of her first boyfriend somewhere near.

Why a creature that beautiful would try so hard to mimic the likes of a man, Dirty could not understand.

But she was who she was, and that was that.

For a woman, Queeny had an impeccable swag. She dressed in the trendiest of urban fashions, drove around in a platium-colored Range Rover Limited, and wore more jewelry than the local rappers and actors. But, it wasn't all glitz and glamor with Queeny. She rode around with a twenty-one-shot chrome Beretta holstered on her side and didn't mind using it.

$$$

Inside of an old garment factory located on the city's Northeast side, Queeny and two Italians—the Vespucci brothers, Frank and Giovanni—were inside conducting a drug deal. Dirty had chosen to accompany her, but she wished he hadn't. Frank and Giovanni were haggling for better prices on the Ecstasy Queeny was selling them, and Queeny was getting upset. Things were about to get ugly, and the less witnesses the better.
"Three bucks per pill sounds a little steep, hey?" Freddy, the taller of the two brothers asked.
"If I'm sellin' junk, yes. Quality product like mine, no. The streets are flooded with bullshit *E* right now. You'll corner the market."
 Giovanni, the stumpier of the brothers, smiled and ran a hand over his slicked-back haircut. "Hey, sister, we ain't lookin' for no teachin'. We only lookin' for the product. And two per pill sounds a lot more feasible than three, no?"
Queeny dropped her head and bit down on her inner lip. "Freddy, I thought we already discussed this?"
"Yeah, we did, but..." Freddy responded.
"But what?" Queeny fired back.
"But we and the family..."
"The family? The family?" she laughed.
"Yeah, the family. As in the outfit, the mob."
     "And you're serious?"
     Giovanni stiffened his face. "As a bomb in a baby carriage, hey."
Queeny erupted in a loud cackling laughter that set Freddy and Giovanni on fire.
"Hey, yo', Queeny," said Freddy, "it wouldn't be a good thing for you to keep laughin', if ya know what I mean?"
Queeny pressed her lips together tightly. "And what if I do?"
Freddy looked at Queeny and retorted, "One might take it as disrespect."
"Yeah," added Giovanni. "And yous don't wanna disrespect the fam..."
In the midst of Giovanni's sentence Queeny went berserk. She ripped her Beretta out from its holster and aimed it at Freddy and Giovanni.
 "Queeny, no!" exclaimed Dirty. "No!" he yelled and reached out for the gun. Queeny sidestepped Dirty and fired a single round at Freddy and Giovanni. She missed but they dropped to the ground instinctively.

$$$

Dirty grabbed her by the arm just after she fired the shot. "What the fuck are you doin'? You try'n'a get us killed? Didn't you hear these muthafuckas say they wit' the mob? Fuck you thinkin'?"

"The mob? Those spinach-eatin'-muffuckas ain't connected."

"And how the fuck you know?"

"Ain't no fuckin' mob in D.C., nigga. Those muffucka's counterfeit!" Dirty looked down at the two Italians as they lay with their stomachs on the ground with their hands on top of their heads, shaking profusely, and Queeny's truth hit him on top of the head like a steel anvil. Freddy and Giovanni Vespucci were not constituents of the mob. They were two shams just as Queeny portrayed, and for that, Dirty thought, they deserved whatever treatment Queeny dished up for them. Be it robbery, death, or both. Luckily, for the Vespucci brothers, anyhow, Queeny settled for a simple robbery. She forced Freddy and Giovanni to strip down to their drawers, tied them to a steel beam inside of the factory, and stole their money. She was cold.

$$$

Dirty sat in the passenger seat of Queeny's Range Rover, sober as an onion as she maneuvered through D.C.'s evening traffic. Queeny on the other hand, was high as shit. She'd dropped enough Ecstasy and snorted cocaine to suffice three people for three days, and, so it seemed, the day had just started for her. She gritted her teeth agitatedly while she drove, occasionally pounding her fist against the steering wheel. "Yo', don't this nigga remind you of 2Pac," she yelled to Dirty, over the grim bassline of Jim Jones's "Don't Forget About Me" single.

Dirty didn't respond. He was slumped over in the passenger seat, thinking about the lady and little girl he had killed. Their deaths were starting to devour him from the inside out. No matter how hard he tried, he couldn't remove the memory from his mind, the looks in their eye's, the blood-curdling scream the child let out just before she died. The images had stained his brain.

"Young?" Queeny called out to Dirty. "Young?" she said and softly tapped him on the left shoulder.

Dirty jumped in his seat. "Ye-yeah? What's up?" He hadn't even realized they had stopped.

"Damn, you a'ight, Family? I know you ain't worried 'bout those greasy-ass whiteboy's back at the factory. Are you? 'Cause if you want we can..."

"Naw... It ain't that, I just... It's a long story."

"Um. Well, if you wanna rap 'bout it later, just say the word. I'm here for you, Young."

"I appreciate it."

"No doubt."

Dirty looked up at the modest peach and white trimmed house and asked, "Where we at?"

"Oh, this my people crib. Come on in and meet 'em."

"Dirty looked up at the house and then back at Queeny. "I'm good. Gotta lotta shit on my mind right now. Probably better if I stay back."

"Probably better if you stay back? Nigga grab the cream and come on… We'll be waitin' on you."

Dirty looked down at the black gym bag between his feet. When he looked back up, Queeny was standing on the front porch, waving him up. Dirty shook his head, sighed, grabbed the bag from the floorboard, and walked up to the front door.

When Dirty walked inside the home, Queeny and a shapely dark-skinned woman with short, stylish hair were locked in a passionate kiss. She wore pink boy-shorts, a white tank-top, and fuzzy pink houseshoes. She and Queeny parted when Dirty entered.

"Dirty," said Queeny, "Dis my boo, Diamond… Diamond, dis my man, Dirty., He from Ohio…"

Diamond smiled as she wiped the essence of Queeny's kiss from her lower lip. She gave Dirty a once-over. "He's cute, babe. I'm feelin' that Mohawk."

Dirty smiled. "Thanks."

"You gon' be in town awhile?" Diamond asked Dirty.

"Yeah, for a couple months maybe."

Diamond licked her full lips and looked over at Queeny. "Um. You may hav'ta leave him with me for a couple hours, babe."

Queeny smiled. "Some other time," she said. "Right now we on business." Queeny grabbed the bag of money out of Dirty's hand and handed it to Diamond. "Here, take this…"

"And do what with it, put it in the safe?"

"Yeah. But count it first, and text me the total."

"Okay," she said sweetly.

"I'll be back later on tonight. Keep it wet for me."

Diamond smiled, spun around and sashayed off towards the back room.

"C'mon Dirty. We got business to take care of," Queeny said as she held the front door open for him.

After leaving Diamond's, Queeny took Dirty along as she visited nearly a dozen drug houses throughout the city collecting front-money from her workers. This gave Dirty an in-depth visual into her operation. Either Queeny was terribly stupid, or she really trusted him. Dirty chalked it up as trust.

After visiting her last employee, Queeny pulled into Alexander's strip mall and cut-off her engine. She set fire to a plump blunt of Kush, and leaned back in the leather seat. Dirty watched her closely as she inhaled the thick white smoke.

"Hey, Queeny… You ever thought 'bout easin' back, gettin' out the limelight?"

Queeny exhaled smoke through her nose before responding. "Like easin' back and lettin' somebody hold shit fo' me?"

"Yeah. Like playin' the back, runnin' shit from behind the curtin."

Queeny smiled. "What, and let you run shit?"

Dirty smiled back. "Nah, not necessarily me… But definitely somebody loyal."

"Naw, I ain't neva thought about it. What make you say that, though?"

Dirty reached out for the blunt. He took two tugs and passed it back. "It's just… Well… To be honest, I don't see a broad runnin' shit for too long. I mean, yeah, cats respectin' it right now—you puttin' in work, what you expect. But be realistic. How long you think that shit gon' last? How long you think niggas gon' accept a bitch runnin' the city streets?"

Queeny puffed the blunt a few more times. "Shit, they gon' keep acceptin' it as long I keep puttin' in work. Dirty… you know how long I been doin' this shit?"

"How long?"

"Goin' on fifteen years. And you know how long I been puttin' in work? Fifteen years. See, I know how niggas think. Niggas only respect one thing: bloodshed. I been deadin' cats like Freddy and Giovanni Vespucci since I was seventeen. That's how I earned my respect, and that's how I'ma keep it.

"And I respect that, I do. But seriously, how long you think that shit gon' last, Queeny? Niggas got too much pride to be gettin' son'ed by a broad… And that bloodshed shit only gon' get you so far, Ma'… I'm serious… I know niggas that'll kill an entire family for ten *G*s cash, and this in Dayton, Ohio. It's much more opportunities for niggas like that here."

"So what you sayin'? You tellin' me to bitch up and tuck my tail between my legs?"

"I'd never disrespect you like that. But, I will say you need to wake up."

"Wake up?"

"Yeah. Wake up, baby. Good things don't last forever…"

$$$

As Dirty spoke, Queeny noticed a black Phantom with darkly tinted windows in her rearview. The luxury vehicle eased up beside her and stopped. Queeny didn't panic. She calmly grabbed the Beretta from her lap and pressed it against the driverside door of the Range.

The back passenger window of the Phantom rolled down, and there sat Omega, Queeny's former business partner.

Queeny rolled down her window as well.

"Long time no see, Queeny," said the massive stretch of man, whom strongly resembled the rapper Rick Ross, with his bald-head and thick beard.

"Sure is. Ain't seen you in quite a while."

"Yeah, I know. Been vacationing, Turks and Caicos to be exact."

"Is that right? Was Team America there?" she asked, sarcasm clear and evident in her tone.

"Team America? Who the fuck is Team America?" Omega asked, puzzled.

"The Feds. Were they with you?"

"The Fed—what?"

Queeny leaned up and out of her window. "The Feds, nigga, the Feds. Did you see any federal agents while you were out."

Omega gazed at Queeny with squinted eyes. "You callin' me the police?"

"I'm sayin' I don't know what the fuck you are. First I hear some Baltimore niggas snuffed you out, then I hear the Fed's got ahold to you? It's obvious the story about the B-More niggas ain't true, so mabye..."

"Watch what the fuck you say, Queeny. You know me... You know exactly how I get down."

"I don't know shit!" Queeny blasted.

"You know I'll send more bloods at that ass than those maxi-pad's you wear."

"Fuck you, you bitch-ass nigga, suck my dick!"

Omega smiled. "That's your problem, Boo. You wanna be a man so fuckin' bad that it irks you. But guess what, you'll never be a man, no matter how hard you try. You'll never have a big black dick like this."

Queeny couldn't take it anymore. Omega's words had burrowed underneath Queeny's skin. Queeny raised her weapon and pointed it at Omega. "I'll kill you nigga! I'll fuckin' kill you!"

Omega didn't say another word. He raised his hand and signaled his driver to pull off.

Chapter Twelve
The Snake, the Rat, the Cat, the Dog

Special Agent Frank Shehee tailed Nicholas "Nino" Humpreys for two weeks—day in, day out. The result of the investigation was a success. Agents seized dozens of kilo's of Cocaine, as well as thousands in cash. Several were arrested.

Humpreys and a female companion were sitting at the kitchen table when fourteen highly trained agents swarmed the house. Cocaine and a silver handgun lie in plain view. Shehee waited for the perfect time to give the signal. The gun on the table created a huge risk. As soon as Humpreys stood up and walked to kitchen sink, Sheehee gave the signal. "Blue team, go, go, go!"

$$$

Nino was at the kitchen sink sniffing water—a trick used by sniffers to expedite the drain process and rush high—when masked agents stormed in on him. "D.E.A.!" one agent yelled, "On the ground, now!" shouted another.

Nino darted back to the kitchen table and grabbed his 9mm automatic.

"Drop the gun, Humprey's!" yelled an agent with a riot pump shotgun in his hand. "Drop it before I..."

Nino slung the gun over his left shoulder and pulled the trigger, sending three hydrashock slugs from the barrel of his gun into the agent's chest. Before the agent hit the ground Nino had ducked off into the laundry room and burrowed himself between the washer and dryer components. The agents immediately returned fire.

Smoke from the bullet-riddled walls made it virtually impossible for Nino to see. The agents were likely equipped with night vision and infrared beams. There was no way Nino was going to make it out of there alive.

"Mise well go for what I know!"

Nino raised his arm above the dryer unit and let off two more shots.

Once again, the cops returned fire.

"Hold your fire... Hold your fire!" Nino heard. "Mr. Humpreys, I'm alive... This is Agent Frank Sheehee, I'm alive... You don't have to do this... Just come out with your hands up... If you give up I can assure you we will..."

"Fuck you, pig!" Nino yelled back and let off three more shots.

The cops returned fire.

"I said hold your fire, damnit! We need this guy alive."

"Kill me muthfucka's! I ain't goin' out like that!" Nino said just before he let off two more shots.

This time the agents didn't return fire.

$$$

After the flashbangs and smoke bombs, Nino was no more good. He thought they'd give him the ass-kicking of his life when they finally placed hands on him, but surprisingly, they didn't. Sheehee apparently had bigger plans for him. He wanted to turn Nino into a rat. And Sheehee's bartering tool? A laundry list of felonies ranging from attempted murder on a cop all the way down to weapons under disability. With Nino's rap sheet, he was looking at a minimum of thirty years behind bars.

There's no way I'm doin' all that time.

"What do you want me to do?" Nino questioned Agent Sheehee.

"We want your supplier. We want Timothy "Tek" Thompson. Give us Tek and we'll let you off with a simple possession. You'll do two years on bond, two years on house arrest, and we'll write it off as four years time served. How does that sound?"

"Its sounds too good to be true."

"Well, it's not. It's one hundred percent legit."

"And just like that, it's done. All of it? The shootin', everything?"

"Everything. As long as we get Tek."

"And I won't have'ta do this no more?"

"Hun-un. No more information on your behalf. Everything's sealed."

Nino shook his head. "Sheeze. You muthafuckas must really want that nigga, huh? What, y'all got a personal vendetta against him or something?"

"Something like that," said Agent Sheehee. "Now, is it a deal or not?"

Nino looked around the room at the D.E.A agents crammed in the room. He hated himself for what he was about to do, but at the end of the day it was better, Tek doing thirty years rather than him. He looked Sheehee in the eyes and very flatly said, "Deal."

$$$

On his regular re-up day, Nino showed up at Timothy "Tek" Thompson's front door accompanied by undercover D.E.A agent Maurice Booker. Booker was dressed to fit the part of a drug dealer—he wore baggy jeans, Timerberland boots, and a green doo-rag covering his head. Booker's service weapon and the marked cash he was told to bring along for the sting was in the trunk of his vehicle. The show had started.

Tek answered the door just before Nino and Booker walked off. He wore maroon jogging pants and a white t-shirt. He clutched a black

Tek-9 in his right hand.

"What up, Tek?" said Nino with a phony smile on his face, extending his right hand towards Tek.

"What up?" Tek asked. "First off, why you ain't call; and secondly, who the fuck is dis goofy nigga wit' you?"

Nino looked over at Booker, then back at Tek. "Oh, he's cool… This my nigga Rico, from the Cincinnati."

"Rico? From da Cincinnati? Yeah, well, what the fuck he doin' here?"

"I uh…" Nino stammered. "I thought we could..."

"You know I don't do company, Nino. And I definitely don't do new faces. Get this nigga off my porch fo' shit get ill."

Booker saw an opening. "It's cool, Fam'," he chimed in. "My name Reek-B, from the 'Nati," Booker said with his hand extended, attempting to give Tompson dap.

Tek looked down on him. "Yeah, I heard him the first time… But like I said, I don't know you, and I don't deal wit' niggas I don't know. Now get the fuck off my porch befo' you get served. I done told you once, if I have'ta tell you again I'ma..."

Nino stepped closer. "Tek, my nigga, he good people, I swear… How long it's been since you known me?"

Tompson paused and thought. "'Bout fifteen years, why?"

"Outta those fifteen years, how many times I bring some bullshit yo' way?"

"None."

"My point exactly. I respect, Tek. I know you don't play no games. I'd never bring somebody to you that I wouldn't pitch to myself."

"So why you ain't pitchin' to him?" Tompson asked.

"Can I be honest? This nigga movin' too fast for me. It started out with two keys. I covered that. Then, he call me askin' fo' four… I handle that. Then, it's five… The next thing this nigga gon' be callin' me talkin' 'bout he want a ten pack. I can't cover that shit, T, and you know it."

Tompson looked at Booker with contempt. "So you vouchin' for this nigga?"

"Do I vouch for him? Of course I do, this my mans."

"Nino, you know I know where ya momma live, right?"

"Man I know how this shit go. You ain't gotta worry 'bout nothin'. He good people."

Tek looked over at Booker, who had just lit a cigarette, then back at Nino. "I'ma rock wit' you on this one, Nino. Don't let me down."

"This nigga cool as the other side of my pillow, Tek."

"He better be, Nino; he better be. If he ain't, that's yo' ass…"

Tompson looked over at Booker. "Hey," he said, "put that cigarette out... I don't allow smokin' in my crib."

Chapter Thirteen

D.E.A. Interrogation Room

D.E.A agents seized over 240 thousand dollars from the residence of Timothy "Tek" Tompson that day. Of that, 120 were marked bills given to him by Agent Maurice Booker. D.E.A agents also recovered sixteen kilos of cocaine, a kilo of uncut heroin, three thousand Ecstasy pills, and a cache of weapons.

Tompson was hauled off to county lock-up and booked on twenty-two felony charges.

The interrogation lasted only thirty-eight minutes.

$$\$\$\$$$

"Listen up, Tompson… Or, Tek as they call you in the streets," said Agent Sheehee, "We've finally got you. You're done. We've finally got you."

Tompson looked at Sheehee and smiled. "Sure I am. Just like the last time, huh?"

"I'm afraid the last time was a little different. You beat us the last time," Sheehee admitted, "but you definitely won't do it again."

"I'ma beat you pigs every chance I get."

"And how is that, Mr. Tompson?" Sheehee asked.

"Because, police never take their time. Just like with the last time. I sure you all thought y'all dotted all your *I*s and crossed all your *T*s, huh?"

"I have to admit, the invalid warrant thing was a good trick," said Sheehee, "but you'll never have another chance like that. This time we *did* dot all our *I*s and cross all our *T*s."

"Is that right?" Tompson said, his words filled with sarcasm. "See, that's your problem… You're playin' checkers, while I'm playin' chess. The fundementals and principles are different, Agent Sheehee."

"How so?" Sheehee asked, picking Tompson.

"While you're sitting back contemplating the next move, I'm thinkin' two moves ahead. That's why you'll never catch me."

Sheehee smiled. "Well, the circumstances are quite different this time, Tompson. Not only do I have you on wiretap distributing five kilograms of cocaine to my undercover agent but I also have a signed affidavit from an informant of mine saying that you did so."

Tompson shook his head and mumbled under his breath.

"What cha say, Tompson? Did I hear you say something about you being fucked and you wanting to aide and assist with my investigation in and effort of saving your own ass? Is that what I heard? Because, if so, I could always..."

Tompson slammed his fist against the interrogation room table. "Get me the fuck outta here. Get me outta here now!" Tompson yelled and rose to his feet with his arm cocked back. But before he could strike the agent, Sheehee countered, slamming Tompson into the table in a submission hold. Sheehee cuffed Tompson, radioed for the sheriff's bailiff, and had Tompson escorted back to booking.

Deep down, Sheehee knew Tompson wasn't going to break. Tompson was too stuborn.

$$$

As soon as Tek made it back to booking, he placed the call to Y.B.

Y.B. was a keen youngster whom Tek immediately took a liking to. Tek saw great potential in him. He knew that with the proper amount of guidance and structure, Y.B. would turn out to be a perfect contract killer. With profound interest in guns and ammunition, a face like a child, and a heart as thick as steel, Y.B would make Tek a fortune. And that he did. By fifteen, Y.B. had fulfilled six contracts for Tek. By age eighteen, twelve contracts. By twenty-six, Y.B. had completed a total of two-dozen contracts for Tek—each of them successful.

Time for contract number twenty-five…

$$$

Y.B. answered on the third ring. "Yeah, who dis?"

"Young'n, this Unc'… Shit ain't lookin'… I'm in county lockup."

"Damn. Is it bad?" Y.B. questioned.

"Ugly."

"Shit… Anything Neph' can do?"

"As a matter of fact, it is."

"Say the word and it's done O.G."

"Lemme see… You remember ol' boy K.T that used to rock wit' the homegirl Crystal?"

"Crystal-Crystal?"

"Yeah, Crystal-Crystal."

"You talkin' 'bout the one that just died?"

"Exactly."

"What about him?"

"You know his partner, the one that starred in New Jack City?"

There was a brief pause. "Yeah, yeah… I know exactly who you talkin' 'bout, what up wit' him? You need me to tune him up?"

"Hun-un. I need you to flush that nigga whole radiator," Tek expressed.

"Word?"

"Word."

Another brief pause prevailed. "Say no more, Unc'," Y.B. said. "It's on. Just keep pressin' ya rack, and keep the remote in ya hand. Shit'll look up soon for ya baby."

"That's what I needed to hear."

"No doubt."

"Be careful, Neph'."

"Don't even trip, this what I do…"

Chapter Fourteen
Who Shot Ya?

YB revved the 600cc engine on the ATV once more before sliding the black ski mask over his face. *The quad'll be perfect for the job*, he thought. *Not only will it grant me unlimited road access, but no one will ever see me comin'. Killing this nigga Nino'll be a piece of cake.* He tightened the leather gloves between his fingers, adjusted the revolver in his waistline and remembered Tek's earlier words to him. "Never forget that you're a professional, YB. This shit you doin' ain't no hobby, little nigga, it's your job. We got investors and employers. Take your time. Do it right, and all is well. We the kings of this jungle, YB. These niggas food. Eat up baby, eat up."

With Tek's words in mind, YB took a deep breath and exhaled through his nose. He revved the engine of the quad once more and quickly shifted into first gear.

Time for Nino to die.

$$$

Like any other Friday night outside of Hook's Barbeque and Ribs, the parking lot was jam-packed with patrons and loiterers alike. Upwards of a hundred people stood outside of the establishment—smoking weed and drinking liquor—while another sixty people stood and sat inside, eager to fuel up on last minute bites.

While Nino sat in the driver's side of his new BMW, rolling a blunt of cranberry Kush, Crystal waited inside the barbeque shack for their order to come up. She'd occassionally turn back and flash her big bright smile at Nino through the large picture window in front of the shack. Of course, Nino would recipocate the gesture. He'd smile back and make crazy faces at her.

Nino had just finished rolling his blunt when he noticed a yellow blur outside his driver side window. Naturally, he was startled. Especially given the fact that there were cars parked on either side of him. He turned to the left and saw a masked gunman holding a revolver. Nino closed his eyes just as the gunman pressed the gun to window. The first shot grazed Nino's forhead, the second claimed his life.

$$$

The loud revving of YB's engine caught the attention of nearly everyone that night, everyone except YB's intended target. Nino was too relaxed, sitting in his car rolling a blunt and listening to music.

Heads turned and mouths dropped as the masked figure whipped into the parking lot. A few smart people immediately dove for cover. Others made off towards weapons of their own, but on average the crowd watched as he zigzagged the yellow Yamaha Raptor through the parking lot with the precision of a professional rider. YB simultaneously downshifted and smashed the brake when he reached the driverside of the silver BMW. He yanked the revolver from his waistline, pressed it against the driver-side window, and eased the trigger back. Then again, and again, again, and again. YB leaned into the window of the BMW—to assure that his mark was dead—and then tossed the gun inside the cab of the vehicle.

"Rest in piss, you rat bitch!" YB shifted back in gear, popped a wheelie and rode it clear out the parking lot.

Take your time. Do it right, and all is well… We the kings of this jungle… These niggas food. Eat up, baby!

Chapter Fifteen
Payin' Close Attention to Details

At precisely 3:30 pm, everyday, Officers Sheller, Booker, and Vicars would exit the precinct, board their vehicles, and take off in three different directions. Not this day though. Today, for some strange reason, they were traveling together. Big Jay marveled at the sight. This was the fourth day spying on the crooked cops, and not once before had they broken their system. Something was definitely up.

Big Jay eased out of the parking lot in an incredulously small, yet considerably inconspicuous Honda Accord. He pulled behind two black SUVs and tailed the three to Tiller's Storage Unit, a vast stretch of land outfitted with thousands of units in various shapes and sizes. The SUVs turned left, the cops continued ahead, and Big Jay pulled over and parked.

From where Big Jay was positioned in the vehicle, he saw the cops and their storage unit clearly. He wanted run up, pistol in hand, and kill every one of them. But what would that do? They were into something heavy, and Big Jay wanted to know what.

Hedecided it best if he just sat back and watched for the moment. Good Thing. No sooner than Vicars lifted the door on the stroage unit, the two black SUVs from the precint skirted up next to Vicars'ss Tahoe. The doors flew open and out jumped eight heavily-armed Latinos from the savage street gang MS-13.

Big Jay's stomach dropped. He grabbed his pistol from the passenger seat and crept closer to the action, taking cover behind a stack of pallets, a few yards away.   The Latinos obviously meant business. Seven of them held large assault rifles—with silencers, shell catchers, and bullet proof vests on their chests—while the other man, a short guy with alligator shoes and linen clothing carried a large handgun. He was obviously the leader of the pack.

"Hello, my friends," said the smaller man. "My name is Jesus Edguardo, but I'm widely known as El Capo."

El Capo? Big Jay said to himself. *I know that name… El Capo? Oh, shit! He's MS-13. How the fuck did these guys get involved with MS-13? Oh my God…No, No… This can't be good.*

"El Capo?" Sheller spat. "And who the fuck are you suppose to be?"

"I am the guy whose product you stole."

Sheller inched for his holstered service weapon, but a tall muscular Latino with a large "13" tattooed on his face yelled something in Spanish and shoved his weapon in Sheller's face.

"That, my friend, would not be a good idea…" Jesus said glancing around at his minions. "I'll be more than willing to let them decorate this shelter with your DNA, Mr. Sheller."

"How the fuck do you know his name?" Vicars questioned.

"Don't be silly, Mr. Vicars. I am El Capo. I know everything about you. With the snap of a finger, I can have everyone in your families killed. The three looked at one another.

"What do you want?" asked Booker.

"It is simple… You have my product and I want it back."

Booker attempted to speak, but Vicars quickly cut him off. "Well, we…"

"You have the wrong people. We're police officers, buddy."

Jesus smiled. "You say this word, 'police officer,' as if to say that you are exempt. You are not exempt, Mr. Vicars. Now, please… Hear me out.

"We'd love to sit here and chat with you, El Capiton, or, Moses, whatever you call yourself… But, I'm afraid we have business to take care of, important business. So, if you don't mind…"

"And you think this is a game, hey, Mr. Vicars? You think I am not who I say I am. Well, just to show you that your American badge means nothing to me—Vado," Jesus called out to the large Latino with the embroidered face, "Shoot him."

Vado aimed his assault rifle at Vicar's thigh and pulled the trigger. The shot dropped Vicars instantly. "Ahhhhh!" he yelled gripping his leg.

Big Jay's eyes grew wide. *Shit! He just shot him. Don't kill him… Please don't kill him… Let me do the honors… Let me fry that crooked pig muthafucka!*

"Mr. Vicars this is why MS-13 is the most feared Latino gang in your country. No one is exempt."

Booker glanced down at Vicars's leg and quivered. "Wh—what do you want?"

"To tell you a story."

"A story?" Booker shook.

"Yes, story," Jesus said as he took a seat on Vicars bumper. "It goes like this… A few months back an informant by the name of Khaki provided detailed information to federal authories that led to the arrest of two of my family's most faithful business customers, the Flenory brothers. This information led to tons of our product being taken off the streets, as well as a lot of our family being incarcerated, including my cousin, Felipe."

Jesus paused and fiddled with his weapon. "And, as if this isn't bad enough, before this pig—this rat—Khaki, is placed into witness protection, he leaked the location of my cousin's stash houses. A guy by the name of Maceo killed my cousin's fiancée, stole sixty kilograms of ninety-two percent of our coke, and went into hiding…. This is where it gets good."

Jesus removed a cigarette from his pocket and struck a match. "Now, it would've been a relatively easy task locating our product, had this Maceo character chose to distribute the drugs in large increments—being that each kilogram bore our insignia—but he did not. He was smart. That was, until he got himself killed, and the remainder of our product stolen..."

Jesus took a long drag from his cigarette, blew the smoke upward, and smiled. "Then, then… We get a call from a friend, an associate, saying he purchased two kilos of our product from this guy whose cousin is a cop. We did our homework and, well, it lead to you."

"But, sir, there wasn't anywhere near sixty kilos in there," said Booker

"Even so, you will pay."

"It's impossible. The money's been spent and there's not much dope left. We can try to sell it and..."

"You will repay me with your services."

"Our services?"

"Correct," said Jesus, "Your services." Jesus stood up, threw his cigarette to the ground, and crushed it with his shoe. "Six months ago, A.T.F. raided my sister's home. Two million in cash, as well as twenty-five kilos of black-tar heroin, and a smattering of jewelry—including a rare gem that belonged to my great-grandmother. You will recover it."

"Recover it?" said Booker.

"Yes. Along with the twenty-five kilos of black-tar heroin."

"What the—no way," said Booker. "We'll never be able to pull it off."

"You will or you will die. All of you will die. As will your families. All of you will die."

Sheller looked at Booker. "He's bluffin'. They're just not that strong. We're the fucking police officers, for God sakes!"

Booker looked down at Vicars, who still lay on the ground muttering, gripping his leg in pain. "But there's no way we'll find it. None of us were a part of that task force. The location is usually only shared amongst those who work the job."

Jesus flashed a wicked smile. "Lucky for you, I have people. People who assure me that what you're looking for is in Precinct 5."

Booker looked over at Sheller. "We have to, man. I don't wanna die."

Sheller bit down on his lip and shook his head.

"How do we contact you?" Booker asked.

"We'll meet here. Two days. Same time, same place. Either have everything on the list or your families die…"

Big Jay waited until both the Latinos and the cops pulled out of the storage unit before he scurried from his hiding place back into the Honda.

Patience is a virtue, baby… Patience is a muthafuckin' virture!

Chapter Sixteen
Dem Goons Out Lurkin'

Queeny's cell phone vibrated against her center console. She scanned the number, silenced the call, and continued maneuvering her SUV through light night traffic.

She looked to the passenger side, at Dirty, who sat slumped in the seat, high on Ecstasy and Congac. "Yo'? You high, Young?"

"No doubt," Dirty murmured. "You?"

"High as shit," Queeny confessed. "It's been a long time since I been this high. Omega used to always say, 'Queeny, relax... Live a little. Niggas die a lot, baby."

Dirty said, as he adjusted himself in his seat, "That's deep.... Speaking of dude, you think he somebody to be worried about?"

"Who? Meg? Fuck Meg. He had his chance and blew it. This my city now. The game don't wait for niggas, Dirty… Everyday niggas bagged up—get killed—and what the streets do? They keep movin'. That's what they do. That's just how it goes."

"But you still didn't answer the question: is he somebody to worry about?"

"I mean, yeah, he's somebody to be worried about. But so am I. Omega know that. That bitch know he'd have ta send a whole fuckin' army to take Queeny out. I'm the queen of spades, baby boy… This my fuckin' city."

$$\$\$\$$$

The phone rang twice before Duece, self-proclaimed five-star general of the *Blood's* gang in Washington D.C. answered. "Who dis'?" he dragged in his raspy tone.

"What up Damu?"

"Who dis—Meg?" Duece asked, exhaling a thick cloud of reefer smoke.   "You already know… Been a long time since I heard your voice, blood."

"Damn! Niggas been sayin' a lot of crazy shit 'bout you, baby."

"They crucified Jesus Christ, you don't think they gon' try 'n' nail me to the cross?"   "Word, word. But you a *hunit*, though?" Duece asked.

"You already know how I get down. But how D.C. treatin' you?"

Duece took another drag from his blunt. "D.C.'s a world away from Harlem son, but you know how we get down. Ain't a nigga breathin' gon' stop us from gettin' money."

"Preach," Omega said jokingly.

"You know, that's what us Harlem niggas do… We get money and look good doin' it." The two laughed. "But what's shakin' in your world

O.G.?"

"I gotta cork in my way and I was thinkin' maybe you and a couple of the homies could loosen shit up for me.

"I can handle that. Speak it into existence, Blood."

"You remember home-girl Queeny?" Omega asked.

"Why wouldn't I? That was your right hand for a minute. That's the cork?"

"Yup."

"What's the ticket?" Duece probed.

"I got hunit in cash for anyone who knock that bitch off the map."

"A hunit? Oh, I definitely can make that pop. Anything special?"

"Nah. Just bring me the chain of diamonds off that bitch neck."

"Say no more. I'ma hit you back at this number when its done."

"I'm lookin' forward to the call…"

Three hours later, Duece and four of his most trustworthy shooters set out across town in a black Chevy conversion van. All but Duece were making last minute checks on their high-powered arsenal.

"Who this bitch again?" asked Trans Am.

"I told you," Duece replied. "Her name Mo'Nique. She used to fuck around with Diamond before she became Queeny's bitch. That bitch love to talk. She hold Queeny's stash sometimes."

"Well, call that bitch back and see if she's sure she's comin'," said Trans Am.

"I told you she said the bitch comin'," yelled Duece from the driver's side of the van.

"Well, damn, where this bitch at? We been here three hours already. Do you even believe that bitch."

"Yeah, nigga, I do. She just got off the phone with Diamond, and Diamond say the bitch on her way."

"Maybe that bitch Diamond told Queeny what was up," butted in Red-Head Dre, given his name for the red scarf he always wore over his head.

"Everybody just sit the fuck back and be patient nigga," Duece barked. "The bitch gon' show up."

No more than ten minutes later, just as Diamond had said, Queeny eased up in Diamond's driveway. Duece and his crew immediately began to cover their faces. "Gametime, baby… and remember. No witnesses niggas."

$$$

Queeny's headlights flickered when she chirped her alarm. She and Dirty laughed and giggled drukenly as they headed up to Diamond's front door. Queeny placed her door key in the lock and turned to Dirty. "Hey, Young?" she said with the her hand on the door knob. "You wanna fuck my bitch, don't you?"

Dirty was obviously caught off guard. "Do what?"

"Diamond," Queeny responded through a mischevious smile. "You wanna fuck 'er, don't you?"

"Do I wanna fuck her?" Dirty asked, obviously embarrassed.

"Yeah. Do you wanna fuck 'er?"

Dirty chuckled. "What made you say that?"

Queeny smiled. "Earlier. I saw the way you looked at her. You wanna fuck her don't you?"

"I mean..."

"You can tell the truth," Queeny said with a sligh slur. "I'm good with it. I just wanna watch."

"Do what?"

"You heard me. I just wanna watch."

Dirty leaned back and looked at Queeny, almost as if his eyes and ears were playing tricks on him. Queeny twisted the knob. "What, you never took me for that type?"

"Nah, I just..."

All of a sudden the gunfire erupted. Behind them, a gun fired and the porch light shattered.

"Oh shit, Young! Get down!" Queeny yelled and dove inside for cover. She peeled her Beretta from her hip and jumped to her feet. Dirty was prone next to her, peeling his pistol from his waistline as well.

The shooting sobered Queeny up instantly. Life or death. She let off five rounds towards the approaching gunman and quickly kicked the front door shut, but the shooters were close. They shot vigilantly, their bullets ripping and tearing through plank wood and the drywall of the house, sending debris and smoke into the room around them.

"Who the fuck is that?" Dirty yelled from behind the sofa.

Queeny let off three more shots through the front door. "Omega! I'ma kill that muffucka!"

The door was disintegrating under the rapid fire of the high-powered weapons.

"Fuck we gon' do, Queeny?" Dirty yelled. "They got a army out there. We can't hold 'em forever."

Queeny checked her rounds. "Let me think, let me think. Diamond!" she yelled. "Diamoooooooond! Diamoooooooooond!"

$$$

Duece and his crew sent more than a hundred rounds into the

house before swarming the porch. Deuce motioned for Mont, a stout brown-skinned teenager with long cornroll braids and freckled skin, to kick the door.

"Take it down!" Duece orderd. "Now! Kick that muthafucka off the hinges!"

Mont reacted quickly. He lifted his leg and slammed it against what was left of the front door. As as soon as the door opened, and the interior of the house was visible, Mont attempted to rush inside. He caught two bullets in the chest, sending him flying back out the door.

"Oh, shit! Duece shouted and backed away. "You two, over there!" he ordered. "And you, over here!"

Duece and Trans Am took to the left, while Red-Head Dre and Spyder took to the right The four stood on guard on either side of the shattered door, building the courage to step inside. "Fuck that," said Deuce, "I need this shit. I'm goin' in!"

$$$

Diamond heard Queeny calling her name from the front room. In the beginning, she didn't know what was going on. All she heard were gunshots, and, like any normal person, Diamond hit the floor. As the clamoring progressed, she realized that the shooters were closer than she thought. She also knew they were targeting her home.

After about fifty or sixty seconds of shooting, Diamond swore she heard someone calling her name.

"Diamond!"

Then again.

It's Queeny!

"Baby!" Diamond yelled and rose from the ground and ran towards the hallway. When she peeked her head out of the door she saw Queeny. "Grab the bitch!" she yelled. "Hurry up. Grab the bitch!"

Diamond rushed to the back of her bedroom to the closet. She pushed open the door, moved aside a loose piece of drywall, and grabbed Queeny's Assault Rifle. She flipped the safety—like Queeny taught her how to do—scurried towards the hallway, and raised the gun…

$$$

The gunmen had managed to back Queeny and Dirty into the den, the second room into the home. As Queeny stood with her shoulderblade leaned against the left wall, directly across the room from the splintered front door, Dirty kneeled on one knee across from her. They both aimed their weapons.

Queeny and Dirty began shooting when the first gunman entered. He was fast and bold. Neither of the two hit him. He took cover behind the sofa, safe from their rounds.

"I'm almost out, Young!" Queeny yelled out to Dirty and let off two more shots.

No sooner than Queeny said that, a loud burst of gunfire erupted behind her. "Queeeeeeeny!" Diamond screamed as she let round after round from the Mini-14.

"Diamond?" Queeny answered.

Diamond never saw the shooter behind the couch. While she was busily shooting at the gunmen approaching from the front, he raised up from behind the couch and sent a round into the center of her forehead. Diamond fell to the ground with Rifle in both hands. She let off another five or so rounds on her way to the floor..

"Diamond! Diamoooooond!" It crushed Queeny seeing her love fall to the ground, dead before her knees even hit the floor. They had fucked up, and Queeny was going to kill them all.

"Ah, you fucked up now!" Queeny shouted. "I'ma kill all you muffuckas!"

Queeny could see the eyes of her lover still staring, seeming almost alive, if only not moving or focusing. She was beyond hope and dug deep for desperation, instead. She lunged from her cover to try and reach Diamond and was hit in the leg by a bullet. She fell forward, sliding across the floor to come face to face with Diamond.

"Oh, Diamond," Queeny said as she pried the rifle from Diamond's fingers. "Don't die, baby. Don't die," Queeny cried as she removed the Mini-14 from Diamond's hands. "I'ma get 'em, baby! I'm get 'em! all" she professed as she rose to her feet with the rifle aimed at the sofa. "I'll kill you! Ahhhhh…."

Queeny was thinking with her heart. She rose and started running towards the sofa. She let off ten shots, maybe, before the shooter popped up from behind the sofa and blasted a round through her left shoulderblade, spinning her completely. Queeny let off another five or six rounds before the next bullet struck her in the abdomen. Queeny collapsed to the ground. "It's over," she mouthed to Dirty, "They got me, Young… They got me…"

$$$

Dirty went into shock and flashed back to the day of the robbery, the look on his aunt's face after she got shot, the blood squirting out of her leg all over the place. Dirty's eyes went blank and his ears rang from all the clamor. By the time he snapped out of it, Queeny was on the ground clutching to her stomach and spewing blood from her mouth. Dirty fired two shots at the gunmen and scurried over to Queeny's side.

"They got me, Young," Queeny muttered. "They got me… They… They…"   "Don't die, Ma… Don't you fuckin' die on me… Don't you die…"

"Too late…" Queeny gurgled. "Time to… Time to… Go…"

$$$

Deuce had just finished reloading his carbine when Spyder ran through the front door. "Cover me," Duece whispered. "They're in the kitchen."

Spyder, doing as he was told, started blasting off shots while Duece made his beeline through the house's living and dining room, past Diamond's dead body, into the kitchen. The first thing he noticed when he entered was Queeny lying on the floor, in a pool, her eyes twisted back into her skull. Deuce placed his carbine to her forehead and pulled the trigger. Queeny's head exploded on Duece's pant leg like a water balloon.

Spyder rushed in when he heard the shot. He looked down at Queeny and smiled.

"The pantry," Duece said lowly, pointing at the door. "On three… One… Two… Three!"

Duece and Spyder fired into the pantry wildly.

"Stop, stop, stop," ordered Duece. "Stop!" he yelled with his hand on Spyder's chest.

Spyder looked over at Duece, the barrel of his rifle smoking like a peace pipe, and smiled, wickedly.

"Open it," said Duece. "Now!"

Spyder opened the pantry door with the barrel of his weapon.

"What the fuck?" he said as he found nothing but punctured cans of vegetables and dry cereal.

"Where the fuck did he…"

Suddenly, a cool breeze swept the back of Duece's neck. He looked up at the small window above the sink. "Fuck! He got away. Shit!"

"Who was he?" Spyder asked.

Duece didn't respond. He walked over to Queeny's blood-saturated body and kicked it. "You stupid bitch! Why couldn't you just lay down and die like the rest of the marks. Bitch!"

Duece reached down and grabed the diamond studded emblem from the ground. "Gimme this shit! This Omega's city now…"

$$$

Dirty hid between two large dumpsters until the patrol cars passed. He crawled out and immediately flagged down a cab.

"Where ya headed, buddy?" asked the cabbie, an older white gentleman with bushy eyebrows and thick mustache.

"Just drive!" Dirty said completely out of breath.

"Will do. Anywhere specific?" the man asked, looking at Dirty through his rearview mirror.

"Ten stops…" Dirty said attempting to catch his breath.

"Ten? I'm afraid I'm gonna need a deposit, buddy."

"A deposit?" Dirty asked looking out of the back window.

"Yes, as in a down payment."

Dirty turned and faced the cabbie. "Do what?"

"A down payment."

"Oh. Here…" said Dirty. He handed the man a fistful of wadded up bills. "Will that do?"

The cabbied inspected the bills. "Will do," he said making a sharp turn on an isolated street. "And the first stop?" he asked.

"First Street."

"First Street? No prob'. Six minutes."

After cleaning out Queeny's stashhouse, Dirty checked into a motel and waited for dawn so that he could rent a car. The teller at the rental agency asked Dirty if would be taking the car out of city limits.

"Yes. Ohio."

Chapter Seventeen
Pigs in a Blanket

The bullet tore completely through Vicars'ss left leg. When asked by the nurse how his injury occurred, Vicars lied.

"My weapon discharged during cleaning," he said.

The doctor ordered Vicodin for pain, stitched up the wound, and sent him home with strict orders to stay off his leg. Pretty shitty that he couldn't be hands- on with the whole precinct deal, but Booker and Sheller seemed to not need him much anyhow. *And besides,* Vicars thought, *it only takes one person for the job. Sign the freaking log, locate the goods, sign back out. Simple as that.*

But it would never be that easy. The three sat outside the precinct in Vicars'ss Tahoe debating as to who'd play what role in the heist.

"Now, hold on, Booker," said Sheller. "It doesn't take the two of us to go in there and you know it."

"Yeah, you're right. But I'll be damned if I go in there and do everything by myself. Especially when you're the one who pulled the fucking trig…"

"Now wait one minute guys," Vicars interjected, "We're in this shit-hole together. There's no need for finger pointing."

Booker scoffed. "Easy for you to say."

"And what is that suppose to mean," asked Vicars.

"It means you're on paid sick leave."

"And?" Vicars fired back.

"And the entire fucking precinct would probably find it quite strange if you go waltzing in there askin' for access to the evidence locker," said Booker.

Vicars raised his middle finger. "Fuck you, Booker. You act as if I wanted a hydrashock in my leg."

"No, fuck you, Vicars!" Booker blasted from the back seat of the SUV. "You almost got us killed with your macho-man bullshit."

"Yeah, well, someone had to step up," said Vicars. "Your black-ass was scared shitless."

"I should've let 'em kill your racist ass," Booker confessed.

"Won't you try 'n' do it yourself then, bad-ass," said Vicars.

"Uh, maybe I will," threatened Booker.

"Maybe I'll break your black head right now, how 'bout that?"

"Hey!" Sheller yelled. "Enough of that bullshit. You two sound like school girls bickering over pudding pops. We'll both go in, damnit. Book', you sign the sheet, I'll carry the bag, and Vic' you keep at the wheel. Deal? Good. Now C'mon on before we start tryin' to kill one another…"

Sheller was the first to step out. He slammed the door and strutted towards the precinct in his normal swagger. Booker was ten steps behind. They looked like two plain-clothes officers entering the precinct—nothing unusual. But, when they emerged twenty-six mintues later, Vicars could tell the difference in their demeanors.

"Everything go smooth?" asked Vicars.

"Just drive, damnit," ordered Sheller. "Hurry up and drive!"

$$$

Big Jay and thirty of his constituents were held up in an empty storage unit awaiting an opportunity for revenge. Heavily armed and ready to spill blood, Big Jay counted down the minutes as he waited for them to show up.

I pray those pigs show up first... With that batch of heroin I could feed the entire Summit Courts... I'd be the man. No more small time. No more robbin' Peter to pay Paul. I'll own this fuckin' city.

Unfortunately, God didn't answer Big Jay's prayer, because as Big Jay watched through a drill hole in the storage unit door, Jesus' convoy pulled into the storage unit and parked. Approximately seven minutes later, Vicars's eased up in his Tahoe, accompanied by Sheller and Booker.

As soon as Vicars's wheels came to a halt, Jesus' men raised their weapons.

"Friends, friends," said Jesus as they exited the vehicle. "Everything went smooth, hey? My source tells me you guys were in and out within thirty minutes. Beautiful. Now… let's go inside and handle bus..."

"No fucking way!" Sheller said clutching the bag in his hand.

What the hell is wrong with this old man? He's got a deathwish.

"You say no, Mr. Sheller? Is that what you said?" Jesus asked facetiously. "Is there a problem?"

"Fucking right it's a problem," Sheller spat.

"And the problem?" Jesus asked.

"The problem is—the problem is you taking us in there to conduct business when we can conduct it right here."

Booker grabbed Sheller by the arm. "What the hell is wrong with you? You tryin' get us killed old man?"

"Killed?" Sheller fired back. "Killed? And what the fuck you think they're gonna do in there? What? Talk to us?"

Sheller and Booker looked at each another.

"I'm not dying without a fight!" Sheller yelled just before he ripped his semi-automatic service weapon from his hip holster.

Jesus and his men raised their guns, as well did Booker and Vicars; still sitting in the SUV, Vicars drew his weapon and thurst it out the window.

"Guys, guys," Jesus said behind a dozen of his men's barrels, "Don't be stupid. Even if you succeed today, your families will suffer tomorrow. I have given strict orders to kill to..."

Boom!

Big Jay managed to creep up behind Jesus and his men. He aimed his riot pump at at the guy who shot Vicars and gave the trigger a pull. The force from the 12 guage pump blew a hole the size of a dinner plate through his chest.

The war had started, and only the strong would survive…

$$$

Jesus tumbled to the ground and ripped his .50 cal from his holster, focusing his attention on the cops—who were fleeing back to their vehicle. Jesus squeezed his trigger, running towards them, firing shot after shot. The first tore through the grill of the Tahoe, sending antifreeze and white smoke into the air. Another of his bullets blew a 50mm hole through Vicars's—while the money shot hit Booker just above his left eyebrow, blowing a popcan size hole in his forhead, spewing blood throughout the interior of the SUV.

"Oh shit!" Vicars yelled as he tried to turn over the ignition. "Come on dammit! Come on you motherfucker! Start, start, start!"

"Hurry up!" Sheller yelled from the back of the Tahoe, dropping several of the approaching gunmen with his pistol. "They're everywhere, Vic'! I can't stop 'em! Hurry up!"

"I'm trying… It won't—Ahh!" Vicars shrieked in pain as an errant round pierced his leg, inches above the earlier wound. Vicars grabbed the Glock 9mm—fitted with a modified thirty-round extended clip—from his lap and aimed it out the hole in the windshield.
He dropped six Latinos with his first thirty round mag, two more with the second clip, but it was impossible to ward them all off. They're were too many. The most he could do was pace his bullets and pray to the Lord that he be saved.

Big Jay wanted the cops dead, but more than anything he wanted the drugs. He pulled his trigger, vehemently, clearing a path to the Tahoe. Sheller never saw him coming. Big Jay managed to get within two feet of him. He put the barrel of the shotgun to his back and blew a hole in Sheller's chest. There was no doubt he was dead, and before his body even hit the ground, Big Jay was at the back of the Tahoe. He opened the back passenger side door, pressed the gun to the back of Vicars's seat, and painted what was left of the windshield with his guts.

Big Jay grabbed the bag, signaled for his men, and ran for cover.

Chapter Eighteen
Hidden Agendas

Dirty found that much hadn't changed in Ohio since he'd left. Same toilet, same shit. The murder count had risen, but that happened to be a good thing. With homicide detectives out searching for those responsible for more recent murders, Dirty was almost certain the heat would be off him for the killings on South Euclid. Also, with the cops on high patrol, the major drug distributors were going to be shaken up. This would leave the streets open for Dirty and the product he took from Queeny.

The first stop Dirty made when he entered Dayton's city limits was his cousin Gabrielle's house. She and Dirty had remained very close since they were children, and outside of their Aunt Cynthia, Gabby was the only family Dirty had. A couple of so-called cousins were scattered about the city, but no one either side acknowledged.

At thirty-five years old, Gabby was the most intelligent, down-to-earth and understanding woman Dirty knew. A devout follower of the Rastafarian faith, she was a true leader and advocate of the black community. Gabby would always go the extra mile for her people. She'd donate clothing, host food drives, help find shelter for homeless or battered and abused women, she'd even give blood if necessary. She was a godsend.

Dirty telephoned Gabby when he reached the recreation center a mile away from her house. The phone rang twice before she answered.

"Hello?" said Gabby in her soft tone.

"You miss me, cousin?" Dirty asked.

"Desmond?" Gabby questioned, obviously happy to hear her cousin's voice. "Oh my God. Is that really you?"

"What you mean, is it me?" Dirty asked. "You don't know my voice anymore?"

"I mean, it's been a long time."

"Six months ain't a long time, girl."

"It is when you're worried crazy about someone... Boy where you been?"

There was a brief pause.

"Layin' low," Dirty answered.

"Laying low? Boy Aunt Cyn' and I been worried crazy about you—why you ain't call?"

"I, I... just needed some time to myself, Cuz."

"Time to yourself?"

"Yeah. A lil' time to myself. To to clear my head, you know?"

"I guess. So, did you have a nice time?" Gabby asked.

"Not really. How 'bout you? You been okay?"

"Well, aside from calling county jails and checking the Internet every day to see if you were locked up, I guess you can say that everything's been okay."

"What about Auntie? She okay?"

"Yeah. She's better. Crazy as ever. She went back home about a month after everything happened."

"A month? What the—I told that woman to stay gone for at least ninety days."

"Well, you know how she is. That's her home…"

"I know. And I probably should've called, but… everybody's okay and that's all that matters, right?"

"Yup, as long as you're okay."

"Gotta say that," seconded Dirty.

"So… where you at?" Gabby asked.

"Well," Dirty said with a slight chuckle, "actually, I'm right down the street from you."

"Really! Quit playin'."

"I ain't playin'. I'm coming down Burkart right now."

"Aw, ain't that so sweet? My cousin comin' by to give me some love."

"Yeah. Well, that and I need somewhere to crash for a couple of weeks—just 'till I get another place."

"You know my home is always open for you, Des'. Just make sure you keep in mind that I have a son."

"I know Gab'. I'll never put my family in harms way again."

"That's good to know. I'm already dealing with Sonny and he's about to—well, I'll fill you in when you get here."

"A'ight… Open the front door. I'm just down the street."

Dirty approached his cousin's nicely built, two-story, Victorian home—with it's newly paved driveway, white Bermuda shudders, and bay window out front—and honked his horn. Gabby emerged wearing dark jeans and a white cooking apron.

"Cousin," she said flaunting a set of bright white teeth.

"Hey cuz," Dirty said as he stepped out of the sedan and tapped the trunk release.

"You got it?" she asked while wiping her dark hands against the bright apron.

"Yeah, I got it…" Dirty said as he lifted the duffle bag from the trunk. "Sonny here?"

"No, but he'll be here any minute. Probably somewhere runnin' behind Manny, Cashmere, and those other fools."

"You talkin' about the rap group Diamond District? He's still messin' with them?" Dirty asked.

"Yup. And that's the main focal point of our problems around here."

"What you mean?"

"Well, everybody know's that those guys still deal drugs."

"Who?" Dirty asked attentively.

"Those guys in Diamond District."

"You sure? But I thought they were clean?"

"They may be, but the guys around them aren't. Sonny's not."

"And how do you know that?"

"Because, the fool had a bag of crack sitting on the mantelpiece last week?"

"What? And where was Semaj?" Dirty asked.

"Thankfully," Gabby said with a sprint towards the kitchen, "he hadn't come home from school yet."

"Damn, that's ill," Dirty added.

"Tell me about it. I would've lost my mind if my son would've seen that stuff."

Dirty took a seat at the kitchen table and watched as Gabby stirred her pasta. "So, that's what he's doin', Cuz? Sellin' crack?" Dirty asked with a look on his face that suggested he was disgusted over Sonny's actions.

"Powdered crack, heroin, weed... I think he sells it all if you ask me."

"Damn. Whatever he doin', he probably need to slow down," said Dirty. "You see what happened to me. Ain't no future in that shit."

Suddenly, a loud rumble of music interrupted.

Gabby snapped her neck towards the front door. "See!" she said dropping the cooking spoon on the stovetop and storming off towards the front door.

"Sonny!" Gabby yelled, "if you don't turn that damn music down!"

Dirty took an apple from the fruit basket and wiped it on his shirt.

"Woman why you always trippin'?" Sonny asked, his voice growing clearer as he came into the house.

"Because," Gabby blasted, "I told you not to blast that mess out here. Damn you're hardheaded."

"You always overreacting," Sonny said, "that shit wasn't even loud."

"The hell if it wasn't. I heard it all the way down the block," Gabby said as she entered the kitchen. Sonny was on her heels.

"Why do you always—Oh, shit… what up, Dirty?" Sonny said as he entered the kitchen.

"What up, Sonny?" Dirty responded around a mouthful of apple.

"I'll tell you what's up." Gabby intervened, "What's up is this fool still think he's in the ghetto."

"Aw, shit… please… Not this again," Sonny complained. "She always does this."

"Does what, Sonny? Huh? What do I do?"

Sonny hissed. "You read all those Rasta books and shit, and then you come preaching to me about the ghetto and all that other bullshit."

"You see what I have to put up with, Cuz?" Gabby asked. "He's a fool. I have a fool for a fiancé."

Sonny walked up behind Gabby as she stirred her pasta sauce and wrapped his arms around her waist. "So I'm still your fiancé?"

Gabby smiled. "You get on my nerves."

"You still love me?" Sonny asked Gabby as he planted soft kisses on her neck. "Do you?" he asked continuing the seduction.

"Yes, boy," Gabby said shooing him away. "You stink. Get away from me."

"I stink?" Sonny said before smelling himself. "I stink?"

"Yes. That weed smell. Ugh. Get away from me."

Sonny looked over his shoulder at Dirty and smirked. "That's Grandaddy, Baby."

"I don't care what it is," Gabby said and nudged Sonny. "Move, I said!"

Sonny kissed Gabby on her neck once more and turned to Dirty. "So, Dirty… What brings you here, my nigga? Ain't nobody seen or heard from you since that shit jumped off at Auntie's crib… What, you in some type of high water or somethin'? You need us to hide you out? If so, we can always…"

"Boy, shut up!" Gabby said as she stirred her pasta sauce. "You always in somebody's business."

Dirty flashed a nervous smile. "It's cool, Gabby," Dirty said and turned towards Sonny, "I'm good. Everything taken care of."

"So what happened?" Sonny asked.

"I took a lil' vacation," Dirty answered

Sonny laughed out loud. "a vacation, huh?"

"Yeah. A vacation. What's so funny about that?"

"A vacation? Where to?"

"L.A."

"Hmm." Sonny murmured with a look of skepticism about his face. "Well," he said with a clap of his hands, "glad you're back."

"Thanks."

"Fo' sho… C'mon, lets have a drink."

After putting away his things, Sonny led Dirty to the basement, where they spoke freely over shots of brandy.

"You like what I did to the place?" Sonny asked, refering to the improvements made in the basement.

"Hell, yeah. Suede furniture, full bar, slot machines, pool table….Is that a…."

"A what? A seventy-five inch flat screen? Yep. You already know."

Dirty shook his head and gave Sonny a handshake. "Okay, then… I'm definitely feelin' this. When'd you start remodeling?"

"Probably, um…" Sonny said looking to the ceiling, "about four months ago."

"How much you got invested down here?"

"About eighty. I ain't done though. I got a old school Pac Man game on backorder and a couple pieces of modern art I'ma throw on the walls to spice it up a bit."

"Modern art? Boy you done turned the hustle up since I've been gone, huh? You ain't playin' wit' 'em are you?"

Sonny smiled. "Diamond District. I'm wit' D.D.C. now. We goin' global, baby."

"Global? Wit' what, dope?"

Sonny laughed. "Hell naw. I mean, don't get me wrong, there's a couple of us that still get down, but thats only to keep the streets happy. We gon' take over shit, legally… music, movies, books, threads, the works… D.D.C the future, baby."

Dirty sipped his drink. "The future, huh?"

"That's right, the future. We got Ohio in a headlock right now, and the Midwest soon to come. Then it's the East and the West. We takin' over, baby. We fuckin' takin' over."

$$$

(Two weeks later)

Dirty found a posh condo in Centerville, a suburban area located twenty minutes south of Dayton, Ohio, and furnished it with the bare essentials—a bed, a refrigerator, a stove. He opted to keep the bulk of his product and money hidden in the floor at Gabby's home. Of course it was wrong that Dirty did so without Gabby's approval, but, in the end, Gabby was all he had.

Dirty's plan was to filter the product from D.C., through Sonny, in the attempt of making good with Diamond District. Then, once he got all the way in, Dirty would begin implementing change from within. First, Dirty would suggest that everyone go legal—completely disassociating themselves with guys like Sonny. The he'd bring up the idea of relocating to a more business-oriented city, such as Atlanta, Georgia. Next, he'd introduce short- and long-term investing, and then finally, he'd move for CEO.

Life is chess, not checkers… Dirty said to himself. *We think, we plan, we plan, and we plan more… I'ma be the next big name in Hip-Hop… Watch and see… Diamond District is my ticket to the top!*

Both the Ecstasy and coke Dirty inherited from D.C. was of exceptional quality and only made it easier for Dirty to get close to Diamond District. The fact that he was offering it at a cheaper rate than the locals made it even better. Dirty's plan came into fruition within a matter of weeks—literally—and, as it just so happened, while Dirty and Sonny were in the middle of a business transaction.

"How much?" Sonny asked.

"Um… Just gimme twenty-five."

"Twenty-five a key. Damn. I ain't heard dem type of numbers in years."

Dirty smiled. "We family ain't we?"

"Sonny smiled back. "Yeah, yeah… family."

"You already know," said Dirty. "And how 'bout the pills? How many you want?"

"Depends on the ticket."

"Didn't I just tell you you were family? They a dolla a piece."

"A dollar a piece? Shit, gimme ten. You got ten thou'?"

"Of course I do," Dirty said.

Sonny began shaking his head. "You know what, I'ma introduce you to the crew."

Dirty played naïve. "The crew?" he said as he tossed the bag of product to Sonny.

"Yeah. The Team. Diamond District."

Dirty looked Sonny in the eyes. "Oh yeah? What, they throwin' a show or somethin'?"

"Naw. The show ain't 'till next weekend."

"So where we goin'?" Dirty asked.

"Diamond District Studios."

"Diamond District Studios? They got they own studio?"

"*We* got *our* own studios," Sonny corrected.

"Damn. That's what's up. When?"

"Shit, lemme drop this work off, and we can head straight over."

"Cool with me," said Dirty, "I can't wait to meet these niggas…"

Dirty and Sonny were greeted by a cute light-skinned girl with long black hair and slightly freckled skin when they entered the studio.

"Hey, Sonny," she said when the two entered the building.

"What up, Nish?" responded Sonny.

"I'm fine," she said with a twinkle of her cute smile. "Manny, Cashmere, Product, and Governor are in Studio 2… The others are scattered around here somewhere."

"Cool. Thanks,"said Sonny.

"No problem."

When Dirty and Sonny approached Studio 2, a red recording sign above the door alerted the two to proceed quitely. Sonny opened the door and a thick white cloud of reefer smoke billowed out from the room.

No one seemed to pay Dirty and Sonny any attention when they entered the room. Manny, Governor, Product, and their women friends were seemingly too enthralled by Cashmere's freestyle to acknowledge them.

Dressed in denim jeans, a white wife beater, a fitted cap, and dark shades, Cashmere stood in the sound booth holding a pair of headphones to his ears.

"It's Cashmere, numba one bull of da team… Pretty thug, stick up ya mans, turn around 'n' drop ten in ya queen… Nhamean. Yjeah!... D.D.C. Mixtape, volume one… be on the look out for the compilation… Midwest Thugs wit' drugs… I'm out!"

Cashmere yanked the headphones from his head and stormed out the booth. "Y'all hear that shit?" he asked sarcastically.

"Nigga you wrote that shit," Product said with a smile.

"Wrote it?" Cashmere questioned. "Wrote it?"

"Yeah, you wrote that shit. That wasn't freestyle, what you spit… Gov', is this nigga perpin' or what?"

Governor looked up from the leather couch in which he was seated between to beautiful women, one fingering the tips of his lengthy cornrolls, and the other rolling a blunt. "Nah," Governer said very slowly, "It was freestyle. That purp' jus' put my nigga in a zone, that's all."

"Bullshit," Product said. "This nigga writin' on us."

"What? Writing? You mad 'cause you can't fuck wit' me, Product? Huh? You mad cause ya boy got flows?"

"Mad? You can't see me, and you know it nigga," said Product.

"Spit then," Cashmere coaxed. "I know you ain't gon' keep on talkin' me to death. Spit, nigga…"

Product cleared his throat. "This nigga Cashmere trippin', knowin' I got go fo' days… I go apeshit, kidnap his hoe, have her suckin' cock fo' days… Anyway, why would I play, when all I do is sit around the trap soufflin' yay… So many grams on the weight bench Fed's lock me up, neva letta nigga see the light of day… Porsche truck parked outside shittin' on ya box Chevrolet… New V's every time you see me, neck piece shinin' from a block away… It's too many guns, too many bricks, too many choppers, with too many clips… I shoot automatic shells at Cashmere, leave 'em broke, busted, disgusted, dead on his dick… Who want it?"

"Oh shit!" Governor said from the couch. "Cashmere, you gotta redeem yaself on that one."

Cashmere looked at Governor, then to Cashmere, and Manny. "What you think, Manny?"

Manny made a another adjustment on the sound board. "Do what?" he asked.

"I said what you think about the freestyle?" Cashmere repeated.

"To be honest," Manny said spinning a dial and raising a lever, "I wasn't payin' attention… But, you need to work on your vocals."

Cashmere looked around at the others in the room. "My vocals?"

"Yeah, your vocals."

"So what's wrong with my vocals?" Cashmere asked.

"They're bland. You gotta give niggas something to hold on to… You gotta make niggas feel you."

"You don't think niggas could feel that?"

"It was bland."

"Shit, I liked it," said Sonny with clarity.

Everyone suddenly turned to face Sonny and Dirty near the door.

"Damn, what up, Sonny?" said Product.

"What up, Product," Sonny answered.

"Can't call it… How long you standin' there?"

"A couple minutes."

"So you heard my freestyle?"

"Yeah," Sonny said. "That shit was hot, too!"

"No doubt? 'Preciate it… I really do."

Manny looked up from the sound board. "What's up, Sonny."

"What up, Manny?" replied Sonny.

"Gettin' the tracks together for the compilation that's all. Who's that you got wit' you?"

"Oh, this Dirty," said Sonny.

"Dirty?"

"Yeah… You remember the nigga I was tellin' y'all about?"

"Dirty?" Manny said looking up towards the ceiling. "Huh-un. I don't—wait. You mean Gabby's cousin? Yeah, I remember you tellin' me about him. The one wit' the work right?"

Sonny smiled. "Exactly."

"The nigga with the work, right?"

Dirty finally smiled. "Yeah, that's me."

Manny stepped from the booth and shook Dirty's hand. "Good to meet you. I heard a lot about you, Fam'."

"Hope it was good," Dirty said making light of the slightly uncomfortable meeting.

"Nothin' but good," said Manny. "You drink, Dirty?" Manny asked.

"A little bit."

"How 'bout Louie?"

"Louie? Most definitely."

"Cool. Take a ride with me…"

From that day on Dirty was a part of the tapestry that made Diamond District. It took a lot of persistence and loyalty to gain their trust, but in the end it finally happened.

Chapter Nineteen
A Case of Mistaken Identity

Toy hadn't spoken to Razor since the deaths of their mother and her daughter. Razor tried contacting Toy on numerous occasions, but Toy would always avoid him. Finally, she gave in.

"Toy!" Razor pled from the outside of their front door. "I know its hard, Sissy, but you gotta come up outta there. It ain't heathly what you're doin' to yourself."

Toy opened the door but said nothing to her brother. She turned her back, dropped her head, and somberly walked back into the living room and took a seat on the couch.

"I can't believe they're gone, Ramone," Toy said with tears in her eyes.

"I know, but its gon' be a'ight, Sissy... We can't bring 'em back, but at least we know that muthafucka dead too."

Toy wiped her eyes. "Dirty's dead?"

"Yeah he's—wait. Dirty? Who the fuck is Dirty? You mean Maceo?"

"Maceo? Oh my god, Ramone. Please don't tell me you're the one who..." Toy stood up and began pacing the living room floor. "No, Ramone. Maceo didn't do it. Dirty did it."

"But, but... But he was the one talking shit that day."

"He thought you were gonna hurt me, Ramone. Maceo would never do anything to me."

Toy began bawling.

Razor threw his hands atop of his head. "Who the fuck is Dirty, Toy? Who is Dirty?"

Toy didn't answer. She dropped her head between her hands and began sobbing uncontrollably.

"Toy?" Razor called out as he hovered over her. "Who is he, Toy? Toy? Toy? Who the fuck is he!" Razor yelled and began shaking Toy at the shoulders.

Toy stood up and smacked Razor. "He's the motherfucker you robbed!" she yelled.   "Robbed?" Razor asked with a clueless look on his face. "Dirty? Sissy, I ain't robbed no nigga named Dirty."

"You mean to tell me you don't even remember robbing him and shooting his aunt?" Toy asked.

"Robbing him and shooting his—that wasn't me, Sissy. It wasn't."

Toy looked into Razor's eyes with a blank expression on her face. "It wasn't?"

"I never lied to you Toy, and I never will. On Momma's grave I didn't do it."

Toy threw herself into Razor's arms. "I'm sorry," she sobbed. "I'm so sorry, Ramone. I thought…"

"Don't worry, Sissy. It's okay. Just tell me everything you know about this Dirty nigga and let me handle the rest."

Toy wiped her face and sniffled. "Well, he hangs with…"

Chapter Twenty
Death Before Dishonor

Thanks to Jesus and his wonderful product, Big Jay was no longer a smalltime hustler. He became rich overnight. People were OD'ing left and right because of the potency of the uncut product, and with each of them that passsed, Big Jay was gaining infamy…

$$\$\$\$$$

Jesus had his ear to the streets, listening, waiting, for details of his stolen product to surface. He reached out to every fence and major drug distributor in the Midwest, and after approximately two weeks, he got the call he was looking for.

"Jesus?" Eduardo spoke in his heavily accented tone, "This is Eduardo. I have good news for you, Papito."

"Good news?" Jesus asked.

"Yes. We have a lead on your product."

"Who is he?"

"A junkie named Snake."

"And where is this Snake?" Jesus asked.

"Held up on the west side of town," Eduardo replied obediently.

"Perfect," said Jesus. "Give Chico the address…"

Jesus passed the phone and reached for his pistol.

Precisely twenty minutes after Eduardo's call, Jesus and three of his men were pulling into an abandoned garage on Paul Laurence Dunbar street. They exited the SUV and casually entered the building.

Upon entering the dimly lit and muggy garage, Jesus spotted Snake. He'd been strung from the ceiling with thick chains and beat to a bloodly pulp. His clothes, nearly ripped to shreads, barely clung about his black body while blood oozed from fresh lacerations on his head, neck, and chest. Snake's collar bones were nearly torn through his skin, and he groaned as blood streamed from his mouth like injured game.

"Mr. Snake," Jesus said as he approached. "Word on the street is that you know who has my product… I want it back"

Snake spit a glob of blood from his mouth that landed inches from Jesus' green alligator shoes.

Jesus reached out and squeezed a wound on Snake's jawline.

Snake yelled in pain. "Aaaah! Aaaah!"

Jesus applied increasingly more pressure.

"Aaaaaaaaah!"

Blood flew from Snake's mouth, landing on Jesus' handstiched designer shirt.

"Where is my product!" Jesus blasted.

No reponse.

Jesus squeezed harder. "I said where is my product!"

Snakes eyes rolled back in his head as he screamed in agony.

"Tell me! Tell me!" Jesus shouted as he squeezed harder and harder.

"Aaaaaaaaaaaaaahhh! Ahhhhh—okay…" Snake mumbled. "Bi…. Big Jay. I got the dope from Big Jay."

Jesus stepped back from Snake and looked him in the eyes. "And where is this Big Jay?"

"Sum… Summit… Summit Courts. Apar… Apartment 3B… Please let me go… Please…"

Jesus smirked as he removed the razor-sharp knife from his pocket. He flipped open the blade and stepped up to Snake.

"No… No…." Snake screamed as Jesus raised the knife. "Noooooooooo!"

Jesus swung the knife at Snake once and ended his life. He then looked over at Eduardo and said "Call the others… We need everyone we have left."

$$$

Just as the sun began to set, a caravan of black SUVs screeched into the main parking lot of Summit Courts. At the time, four-year-old DeQuan Houston, from apartment 2H, was standing on the sidewalk out front of his apartment bouncing his basketball. His head zipped left to right, as he bounced and counted each passing vehicle.

"Won, two, tree, poor," he announced, bouncing the ball with both hands. "Pie, six, teven, eight, nine, ten, eleven!"

DeQuan dropped the ball and clapped his hands together, estatic that he remembered his numbers.

$$$

Their vehicles swarmed the third and final parking lot of the apartment complex, their tires screeching as the vehicles came to a halt, sending thick clouds of white smoke into the air as the SUV's formed a synchronized V in the parking lot. Their doors flew open and out poured nearly fifty Mexicans with high-powered rifles and sub-machine guns.

Looney and six of his men emerged from an abandoned unit, all holding automatic weapons.

"I'm looking for a guy named Big Jay. He has something that belongs to me… As long as I get it, there will be no problems. If I don't, we are prepared to die here today."

Looney raised his Carbine at Jesus. "Your men killed a lot of our people the other day," said Looney. "They were my family."

"As well as were the individuals who died on my side…" Jesus said gripping his weapon tightly, "but we did not come here to further battle. I only want what belongs to me."

"The diamond?" Looney asked.

"Yes, the diamond. Do you have it?"

"No," Looney said with a shake of his head. "An ex-partner of mine."

"Ex?" Jesus asked. "You mean, Big Jay?"

"Yeah… You know I never understood the saying, "money is the root of all evil until the other day. We put our life on the line, and he repaid us with…"

"What? Dishonor?" Jesus asked.

"No doubt. We lost twenty-one people out there, and he didn't even offer to help pay for their funerals."

"I understand. I do. And believe me, *I* will help. All that I ask is that you give me Big Jay."

"Apartment 3B. He's all yours."

$$$

While Jesus' men swarmed Big Jay's apartment door like mercenaries swarming a bunker in Iraq, Jesus lagged behind. When he made it to the door, Jesus slowly raised his hand and gave the order.

Strike!

Seconds later, Big Jay's apartment door flew open and Jesus' men stormed in.

$$$

Big Jay was on his knees, giving his female companion head in his front room when the door blasted open.

"Oh, shit!" he yelled and threw his hands in the air. The young woman threw herself to the corner of the couch and covered her face with her statuesque legs.

"In my country," Jesus said strolling over towards Big Jay releasing the safety on his .50 Caliber handgun, "we have a saying… '*Ojo por ojo… diente por diente.*' Do you know the saying? It means an eye for an eye, tooth for a tooth."

Big Jay smiled nervously while Jesus looked around the apartment, taking obvious note of all the newly refurbished items; the new sixty inch plasma televisions, the mound of DVDs and gaming equipment, the bags of designer clothing, and cases of Swisher Sweets and Black and Milds.

"Listen, I didn't mean to…"

"Save your breath… You punctured one too many eyes, yanked

out two too many teeth, to aplogize to me, my friend… Today is a day for revenge."

Jesus reached into his pant pocket and removed a syringe, it's barrel filled with dark brown sludge, the needle long and shiny.

"It's, it's over there…" Big Jay stuttered. "The diamond's over there. Take it… The dope, too… There's three ki's left… Please, don't kill me."

"What's done is done. Accept the consequencs of your actions."

Jesus took a step closer to Big Jay. His men rushed in and grabbed Big Jay by the arms, holding him against the couch at gun point.

"I only wanted revenge!" Big Jay yelled. "My beef wasn't even with you."

Jesus walked closer.

"Come on, man… No! Please… Please… No… Noooooooo!"

Jesus shoved the needle in Big Jay's neck and emptied the barrel.

"Fuck you…" Big Jay, said attempting to stand to his feet. "Fuck you all… you-you… you wet-back motherfuckers… I'll… I'll kill… each and every… each and every… I'll kill you all…"

Big Jay's words faded as the heroin traveled quickly through his system, taking over his body. Foam gushed from his mouth, and his eyes turned a whitish shade. His bowels released, he let out a loud groan, and Big Jay took his last breath.

$$$

Jesus walked over to the young woman and tapped her.

"Please, don't kill me," she trembled.

"Look at me," said Jesus, standing inches away from her.

The young woman looked up at Jesus, petrified.

"You-you are too beautiful for this lifestyle…" Jesus said raising the womans chin so that she looked him square in the eye. "Beauty is your gift… Usually I would have you killed here today… You've been granted a second chance… Make good with it."

Jesus took his grandmother's diamond and left the remaining kilos for Looney and his men.

Chapter Twenty-One
I Got What I Came for

Two months had passed since Dirty's first meeting with the Diamond District clique, and thus far, he'd definitely gotten what he had come for. He was dead smack in the center of their firm, and he was loving every minute of it.

Out of the top four—Manny, Cashmere, Product, and Governor—only two were dealing. Cashmere ruled the city with an iron fist in his cocaine and heroin distribution, while Governor controlled the land with exotic reefer and Ecstasy.

And then there was Dirty.

Ultimately, Dirty ended up being Diamond District's main drug supplier. He packaged, distributed, and, on some occasions, collected proceeds for the team. Dirty was gaining heavy recognition for being a team player in the eyes of Manny and the others. Things were going good, but he couldn't shake what he did with Toy. Sure, it seemed as if the case had been pushed to the back of the file cabinet, but all things aren't always what they seem…

It was Friday night and the coliseum was packed. Diamond District was to open for Lil' Wayne and Gucci Mane, and the night was still young. Product had just finished up his verse in the Diamond District anthem. Governor was next.

As the thick white smoke from the background effects began to spew from the machine and onto the stage, Dirty saw what he thought was a familiar face within the crowd. Although only a small portion of her face could be seen—due to the overhead lights and the massive crowd in the coliseum—Dirty could see the chocolate fullness of her lips, and the seductive gaze in her brown eyes.

Dirty moved about the stage, attempting to get a better view of this woman, but with Manny, Cashmere, Govenor and Product all on the stage with him, Dirty would have to finesse his way to her.

When Dirty got closer to the woman, he noticed that everyone but her seemed to be cheering. She was standing still, emotionless, her lips pressed together firmly, eyes squinted.

It was Toy.

Dirty lost his footing when he saw Toy's face, loosing his footing and gaining two left feet.

Fuck! I wonder if she noticed me? She had to… Did she… Wait… Where'd she go? Dirty quickly rushed backstage to collect himself. He set the microphone down and kneeled in the corner with his hands atop his head.

I knew this shit was gonna come back around… What the fuck is she doin' here?… What do I do? Do I stay? Do I leave? If I leave, what do I tell the crew? That I'm sick? That I broke out with some chick? Or should I—

"Mr. Stephens?" the voice called out. "Mr. Desmond Stephens?"

Dirty's heart skipped a beat. He was too scared to open his eyes.

It's a hit… Guess it's my time to go… Please, God, forgive me for my sins… Yea though I walk through the valley of the shadow of death I…"

"Mr. Stephens? Mr. Stephens?"

Dirty slowly opened his eyes and noticed a middle-aged man wearing tan slacks, loafers, and a badge.

Dirty rose to his feet. "Who are you, and what do you want?"

"My name is Detective Dennis Farr and I'm with homicide," he said, placing his hand atop his waistline holstered weapon.

That bitch put the cops on me?

"Homicide?" Dirty asked, appearing to be shocked. "I ain't killed nobody, so what you want with me?"

"Sure you didn't. Anyhow, I have a few questions for you… now, if you don't mind, come with me to the station and…"

"Am I under arrest?" Dirty said bluntly.

"No. Not technically," the detective replied. "But you are under suspicion of…"

"No," Dirty snapped. "I ain't goin' nowhere if I ain't under arrest."

"Afraid of something, Mr. Stephens?"

"Nope. I'm just not going to any police station unless you got a warrant."

"So, you're gonna make me get a warrant, huh?"

Dirty nodded his head. "I guess so."

Detective Farr turned to walk away. "Will do," he said, "but, before I go, you mind telling me one thing, Mr. Stephens?"

Dirty looked at the detective with a blank face. "What?"

"Was it easy killing the girl?" Detective Farr asked before spinning on his heels and exiting backstage.

As soon as Detective Farr disappeared, the curtain leveled and the remainder of D.D.C. came rushing towards him, hyped up from their performance.

Can't let 'em see me sweat… Don't let 'em see you sweat, baby…

"We killed that shit!" said Manny.

"Yeah, nigga! We killed it!" yelled Cashmere.

Dirty smiled and shook hands with his boys.

Manny seemed to sense something in Dirty's composure. With his arm wrapped around Dirty's neck, looking him square in the eyes, he asked. "You a'ight, Fam'?"

"Am I alright? Yeah. Why you say that?"

"You look a little flushed. And I seen the way you broke off stage. What's botherin' you?"

"It's just… My stomach been fuckin' wit' me."

"Your stomach?" Manny asked with his face twisted in a bunch.

"Yeah, I think it's the E. Triple stacks always fuck wit' my stomach."

Manny looked at Dirty strangely. "I guess… Anyway, you wit' me tonight, right?"

"What's next? Dirty asked.

Manny smiled. "After the show it's the after party… After the party its the hotel lobby…"

"An after-party?" Dirty asked.

"Nah. I was thinkin' we'd skip the after-party and move straight to the hotel lobby. Ha, ha…"

Chapter Twenty-Two
Interrogation Room 6

"Okay," said Agent Steele "now you're getting somewhere. For a minute there you were starting to bore me. Hold on a minute…"

Steele flipped his cell phone open. "Yeah. Sure…" he said into the phone. "Still want your lawyer, Johnston?" he asked Pretty Tony.

"That's him?" Pretty Tony asked with a shocked expression on his face.

"No. But, apparently he's downstairs, raising hell. You still want him present?"

"Just tell him I… Just tell him I…"

"Do you want him here or not, Johnston?"

"I uh… I…"

"You know, just patch me through to him," Steele said into the phone. "Mr. Daniels? Is that you? Oh, hello. This is Agent Steele, of the F.B.I. Yes, I do have your client with me… Yes… No, well, sort of… I, well, I'll let him explain…" Steele smiled and passed the phone to Pretty Tony. "Here's you're attorney," he said sarcastically.

"Hello? Clive?" Pretty Tony said into the phone nervously.

"Is that you Tony? What have they done with you? Are you okay? Did they question you? If they did I'll…"

"It's cool. Everything is cool."

"Cool? Where do they have you housed? I've been here for nearly an hour and they claimed you're not in their computer. Where are you?"

"It's cool, Clive. Everything's cool."

"Everything's cool?" Clive asked. "Have they hurt you?"

"No. But I got everything taken care of. You can go back home. Sorry I woke you."

"Go back home? Jesus, Tony, please don't tell me they got to you?"

"It's not like that Clive… I just… I… It's hard to explain."
"So they did?" Clive asked.
"They threatened my family, Clive. I had to."
"Well, you know my rule. No snakes in this clubhouse. If you'll bite one, you'll bite all."

"But it's not like…Clive. I just…."

"Save it, Johnston. The only thing worse than a rat is a pig. And that's because a pig'll eat his own shit… You and I have no further dealings, Johnston. I'll have Kathy mail you a refund for your retainer."

"But I…."

"Watch your neck out there, Tony. Watch your neck."

Click.

Steele smiled. "Everything okay?"

Pretty Tony shook his head and exhaled deeply. "Yeah, man. Let's just get this shit over wit' so I can bounce."

Steele clicked his pen and adjusted the pad on the table. "So… What happened next?"

Chapter Twenty-Three
Generational Curses

Gabby's eyes were red and swollen from crying all morning. At 7:06 a.m., she received the most disturbing call she'd ever received. Sonny was dead. The cops found him slumped behind the wheel with a bullet in his head.

Although Gabby knew such calls were common amongst street guys, she truthfully wasn't prepared for it. She didn't know whether to begin planning his funeral or continue grieving.

At around nine a.m., Gabby called Dirty. "Hello? Des'? It's Gabby. They killed him,
Cuz. They killed Sonny."

$$$

Dirty dropped the bottle of liquor to the floor, grabbed his pistol, and headed for the door. He jumped on his motorcycle and made it to Gabby's in eighteen minutes.

When Dirty entered, he found Gabby sitting on the sofa with a box of Kleenex in front of her. Dirty immediately sat down and hugged her.

"What happened, Cuz?" he asked.

"They shot him in the back of the head. Who would do somehting like that?"

Dirty glanced back towards Gabby's guest room. "Where'd they find him at?" he asked.

"Parked in an alley in Dayton View."

"Cops got any leads?"

Another glance back towards the room.

"No," Gabby said with a sniffle. "They said a neighbor called in to report a strange car in the back of their house."

"What the hell was he doing over there? That ain't like him. Was it a robbery?"

"Nope. They found a large amount of cash and drugs on him."

"Damn," Dirty said shaking his head. "Damn, Sonny. Well, look… I'll help you out with whatever you need."

"It's not about money, Desmond. I need my man. I need my son's father… It's just stupid. It's stupid how y'all line yourselves up at the guillotines and penitentiaries the way you do… You all claim to be men—thoroughbreds, with so much polish—but look what you look like in the end. *Fools.*"

Gabby stood up and wiped her eyes with a Kleenex. "You leave us women behind to raise your kids, to end the generational curses, but its hard, Desmond… It's so hard… We fight tooth and nail but its hard for a woman to raise a good young man… We teach 'em to mind their elders, do good in school, and respect themselves… But as soon as you niggas come around—with your expensive clothes, diamonds chains and your jazzed-up cars—they go astray. They become lost, victims of the struggle, forced to grow up in a world that's cold. I can't let my son become another statistic, Desmond. I just can't."

"So what are you gonna do?" Dirty asked, not knowing what to say, but not wanting his cousin to feel as though he wasn't there for her.

"I'm thinking about moving."

"Moving?" Dirty asked. "Where to?"

"Probably somewhere down south. Atlanta or North Carolina. Somewhere with more opportunities. Dayton isn't right. It's just not right. Too much negative."

"Well, you know I'm with you. Anything you wanna do just let me know. I'll pack up my shit and bounce with you. Okay? I'm here for you cousin. Just say the word and we out."

Gabby smiled.

Dirty gave her a nice snug hug and left her to be alone. As soon as he got in the car he called Manny.

"Hello?"

"Manny? It's Dirty."

"What up? Why you callin' so early?"

"Its Sonny's. He's dead, man."

"He's what?" Manny asked.

"He's dead, man. Dead."

There was a brief pause. "Damn," Manny said with indifference. "That's ill. We'll,. meet up a little later. Stay tight."

Click!

Chapter Twenty-Four
l Got Blood on My Hands Already

The Thursday following Sonny's death, Dirty received a call from Governor. "Meet us at the studio," Governor said. "Ten p.m."

"What's up?" Dirty asked. "Somethin' wrong?"

"Just be there. And don't be late."

"But what's goin'..."

The phone went dead.

Dirty drew back from the phone. *What the fuck? I hope…*

Dirty had been on edge ever since he saw Toy at the coliseum. The death of Sonny only added fuel to the fire.

I'm leavin' this fuckin' place… I don't know what the hell is goin' on, but I can run my show from the road.

Directly preceding Governors call, Dirty began packing. He loaded the most valuable possessions from his condo into his Louis Vitton book bag and headed for the door. Before he left, he removed the safety from his pistol and took a whiff of coke.

As he walked to his motorcycle, Dirty felt as if he was being watched. He quickly ripped the gun from his waist and held it against his right leg until he reached his bike.

The first thought that came to Dirty's mind when he eased out the parking lot was, *As long as I make it off Main Street I'm cool…*

A car suddenly whipped out from the parking garage behind him. *Fuck.*

Dirty glanced in his rear-view. There were several cars on the two lane street, but only one directly behind him.

Dammit, a red light… Too much traffic to pass through… Hurry up and change dammit… Hurry up and change!

Dirty clenched his teeth and revved the 1000 cc engine as the bluish lights flickered towards him.

The black Audi A8 quickly switched lanes and stopped behind a red sports car on Dirty's right side. It's tinted windows made a difficult task of Dirty getting a visual on the driver, but he knew something wasn't right.

Hurry up and change… Hurry up and fucking *change, light… Shit! There it goes!*   Dirty shifted the bike into gear and revved the throttle simultaneously. The bike jolted forward with its front wheel in the air. Dirty twisted the throttle back and rode the wheelie down Main street for another forty feet before bringing it down. But the Audi stayed on his tail.

Shit!

Dirty downshifted and weaved the bike in and out of the night's traffic like a professional, but the driver of the Audi was persistent in keeping up with him. He mimicked Dirty's movements to a tee, maneuvering in and out of traffic, wildly, barely missing other motorists and stationary vehicles.

When Dirty approached Assembly Boulevard, he pulled in on the clutch, dropped the bike into second gear, and made a quick right turn. Shift, shift, shift… within seconds, he was back in fifth gear, riding it high. But the driver of the Audi was still on his tail. Dirty knew he had to make a clutch move. The driver of the Audi seemed just as adamant to catch Dirty as Dirty was at eluding him.

Maybe it's Sonny's killer, Dirty thought. *You'll never take me alive!*

In one swift motion, Dirty downshifted, smashed the front brakes and leaned forward into a frontward indo. He then tapped the brake, put pressure on the seat—bringing the bike down to its normal position—ripped the semi-automatic from his waistline and aimed it at the Audi.

Boom! Boom! Boom! Boom! Boom! Boom! Boom!

White smoke spewed up from the Audi's wheels as it came to a screeching halt. The driver quickly shifted into reverse, spun, and disappeared down a side street.

Dirty sighed and shoved the pistol back into his waistline.

What the fuck is going on?...

$$$

When Dirty pulled up in front of Gabby's he noticed her car wasn't there.

Good. Now I won't hav'ta tiptoe around while I hide this shit.

Dirty scanned the house for anything out of place before walking into her guest room. He moved aside the bed, peeled back the two floor boards he'd loosed and shoved the entire book bag down inside it. He then scribbled a few words on a post-it, stuck it on Gabby's refrigerator and headed for Diamond District studios.

When Dirty pulled into the parking lot of the studio, the fleet of exquisite automobiles out front notified him that everyone was present. He maneuvered the bike between Manny and Cashmere's matching Bently GT Coupes, and silenced his engine.

I hope this isn't anything bad. I can't handle anything else right now...

Dirty tucked the gun underneath his shirt and walked into the studio.

When he entered the conference room, Dirty found that every vital member of the crew was there. He took a deep breath. For some odd reason he felt ashamed; as if he were about to meet a firing squad.

Everyone turned and faced Dirty when he entered.

"You're right on time," Manny said as he stood from the large rectangle conference table in the center of the room. "Shut the door. We got business to take care of."

"What's goin' on?" Dirty asked looking to Manny, Cashmere, then Product and Govenor.

"What's goin' on is we got a Fed in the family."

The information was obviously new to everyone in the room.

"A Fed?" asked Cashmere.

"A what?" said Product.

"That's right," said Manny. "A Fed."

"A Fed?" asked Dirty. "How you know that?"

Manny picked up a glass of liquor from the table and took a large swallow. "You know," he said, "when I started the first Diamond District I vowed not to let any weak niggas around me… No potential liabilties to the firm… No lames… Nobody that'd ruin my dreams… Obviously, it went wrong somewhere."

"Man, you sure you ain't trippin'?" asked Dirty with a nervous smile attached to his face.

"Trippin'?" Manny said looking around at the room at his constituents. "Trippin'? Would you say I was trippin' if I told you there is a fuckin' Fed in this room right now? Would you!" he blasted. "I didn't think so, nigga."

Manny pulled a blue steel 10 mm automatic from his waist and laid it on the table before him.

"But, the five million dollar question ain't who this nigga is, but who let 'em in." Manny looked around the room. "Anybody feel like helpin' me out and tellin' me how this nigga got in? Nobody? Okay, well, let's do it this way… Let's start with the last ma'fuckas to get down wit' D.D.C—Skillz, J-Scheme, Prince, Dirty—how 'bout that?"

Everyone in the room turned their attention to the four members in question.

"Who gon' start?" Manny asked. "C'mon on now. Who gon' brave the waters? Don't be shy. These could be your last words. Betta make 'em right"

J-Scheme stood up from the table. "I ain't no Fed!" said the caramel-complexioned teen with a bald fade and goatee. "Everybody in here know my people—Craig-G, Black, T.T., Lamar from Summit Courts. I never ratted on a nigga, and never will. Shit, I been solid since shitty pampers and Similac. Now I don't know what the fuck goin' on, but I ain't got nothin' to do wit' it."

"Who brought you in J-Scheme?" asked Manny.

"You brought me in," J-Scheme answered matter of factly.

"And how'd we meet?"

"Shit, you approached me on the block—on Paul Larence Dunbar and Riverview—and asked me if I wanted to get cash wit' you."

"Hm," said Manny turning to the remainder of his crew. "And then there were three…"

Manny looked over at Skillz, a twenty-five year old aspiring R&B artist with a nack for writing music, and asked, "What about you, Skillz? Who put you down?"

"Cashmere brought me in."

"Okay, okay," Manny said shaking his head. "And where'd y'all meet?"

"Umm… He got my number from Product."

"Oh, so you know Product too, huh?" Manny quizzed.

"Yeah. I write hooks for him all the time."

"So what happened when you he gave Cashmere your number?"

"Cashmere hit me up, we linked up for drinks, and I started writin' for him."

"You bring anybody else in?" asked Manny.

"Nope. Nobody."

Manny looked around. "Well, guess that speaks for Skillz… And then there were two." Manny looked at Dirty and then to Prince. "Which one of y'all niggas wanna go first?"

Prince—a self-procliamed pretty thug—stood up and fanned his hand about the room. "First off," he said, "I don't owe none of you niggas no explanation. But, I understand the seriousness of this shit, so I'ma keep it *G*.

Manny twisted up his face. "Nigga miss us wit' all that fake tough shit. Just tell us how the *fuck* you got down."

Prince squinted his eyes and clenched down on his teeth at Manny.

"Well, we waitin' nigga!" blasted Manny.

"Nigga!" Prince yelled, "I gravitated towards niggas that gravitated towards me."

"You gravitated towards niggas that gravitated towards you?" repeated Manny. "What the fuck that 'posed to mean?"

"It mean just what the fuck I said. I gravitated towards niggas that gravitated towards me. It mean hard work and dedication got me in."

"Hard work and dedication, huh?" Manny asked sarcastically. "Yeah. I beat those fuckin' streets up—weed, coke, CDs, T-shirts, whatever needed to be sold, I sold it. While you niggas was held up in Five Star hotels, kickin' ya feet up—Manny, Cashmere, Governor, Product— where was I? Where was Prince? I was in the trenches wit' rats and roaches, pushin' your shit, that's where I was. But what about this nigga right here," Prince said pointing at Dirty. "This the nigga y'all need'ta be checkin'. This the nigga who shit ain't addin' up."

Dirty took two steps towards Prince. "Nigga, what?"

"You heard me. You were the last one to come into this shit. We need ta be checkin' yo' muthafuckin' resumé."

"And what you sayin'?" Dirty fired back. "Your try'n'a say I'm a…"

"I think it's obvious what he's sayin'," Manny cut in.

Dirty whipped his head back towards Manny. "And you ridin'

wit' this nigga, Manny? You think I'm a Fed?"

"I think shit just ain't addin' up."

"Shit ain't addin' up? Fuck you mean?"

"I mean," Manny said walking closer to Dirty and Prince, gun by his side, "we meet you what, four months ago? Through Sonny, a nigga that's dead?"

"Yeah, and so? That nigga gotta baby by my cousin."

"I know… But, you come to us with a shit-load of product, and not once have any of us saw you cop, or know anyone that you may've copped from."

"So? And that makes me a Fed?"

"No, but it does raise suspicion."

"Suspicion? Man I…"

Manny cocked the gun and aimed it at Dirty's head "You wearin' a wire, nigga!"

Dirty fell back against the wall and covered his face. "Oh, shit! You trippin', Manny!"

"Naw, nigga. You trippin'. If you ain't wired, fuck you scared for?"

"What I'm scared fo'—you holdin' gun to my head."

"Lift ya shirt, nigga! Lift ya shirt!"

Dirty obeyed, exposing his tattoo-covered chest and stomach. "That's what you wanna see?"

"Yeah, nigga!" Manny yelled back. "We wanna know you ain't a Fed'. Prove to us you ain't no fuckin' Fed nigga."

"Prove it? How the fuck I'm supposed to—nigga you know me! Manny you fuckin' know me!"

"The only thing I know is if you don't prove me wrong you gettin' a hydrashock through yo' melon. You got ten seconds… Nine, eight…"

"C'mon, Manny, you ain't gotta do this!"

"Six…"

"Shit, man, I…

"Five, Four…"

"Please man I…

"Three, two…

Manny cocked back the hammer. "One… say goodbye, nigga."

"Alright, alright!" Dirty yelled. "I got blood on my hands, dawg!"

"Say what?" Manny said with the gun at Dirty's temple.

"I said I got blood on my hands already, dawg!"

"Fuck that mean, you got blood on ya hands already?"

"Those two bodies, on Euclid… The woman and the little girl, that's my work."

"That's yo' work? You sayin' you put 'em down?"

"Some niggas robbed me… shot my aunt, took five hunit in cash… I took care of my business and shot to D.C."

"D.C.?" Manny asked with the gun pressed against Dirty's forehead.

"Yeah. I was gettin' my money up when some niggas ambushed me and the plug."   "What about all the work?"

"My connect had shit clickin' in D.C.. I hit her stash and bounced."

"So, that's where all the product came from, huh?"

"Yeah, bruh. It's all real. I ain't no Fed, dawg. If you want to, you can call and check wit'…"

In a swift motion, Manny removed the gun form Dirty's head, aimed it at Prince and pulled the trigger. Prince's body hit the ground with a loud thud. Blood poured from the gaping half-dollar sized hole in the center of his forehead like a water hose.

"What the fuck!" Dirty yelled. "Why'd you…"

Manny smiled. "Guess everybody know who the Fed is now, huh?" he said hovering over the bleeding corpse.

"But how'd you…" Dirty stammered. "You just…"

"Gotta call the other day," Manny said as he reached into his pocket and removed a picture. "My chick's gotta aunt that's a secretary for the A.T.F. She told me they built a joint task force six months ago to take us down. I asked her to email me a picture of the Fed on our case, and, low and behold, it was Prince—or, Special Agent Nicolas Pendergrass."

Manny tossed the picture on the agent's chest and spit on him. "And how did he get in?" he said rhetorically. "Sonny. And where is Sonny right now? In the casket where he belongs."

Manny waved the gun across the room. "Now, let this be a lesson… The penalty for deception around here is death… Let no man destroy what we hand-built… Diamond District!"

Chapter Twenty-Five
99 Problems, and the Clip Is One

Razor was out to get revenge for the deaths of his mother and niece, and he wasn't going to stop until he had Dirty's head on a platter.

Razor's first stop to locate Dirty was a local weed and pill house located on the city's west side. The place was owned and operated by Diamond District, so Razor figured that'd be the best place to start.

The establishment was run like a beer and wine drive thru. You'd pull your car down the alley, ease up near the old rickety dwelling, honk your horn, and seconds later one of Diamond District's young employees would lean out the window and take your order.

Razor prayed Dirty was around. He'd kill him, ride off, and put everything behind him for good.

Could be the easiest job I ever pulled in my life…

Razor pulled back the slide on his Mac-11 as he turned into the alley leading to the establishment. He covered the weapon with his T-shirt just as he eased up to the brown and white shabby building surrounded by empty liquor bottles and potato-chip bags. When he honked the horn a brown-skinned youngster with spotty skin and a black fitted cap opened the window.

"What up, Fam'?" he said showing a mouthful of gold teeth. "What you tryna get?" "Aw naw, I'm lookin' for Dirty."

"Dirty?" the youngster said, with a look on his face that suggested he was trying to place the name with the face in his head. "Oh, he don't come 'round here much. I got you tho'."

"You know where he at?"

"Nope," replied the youngster. "Maybe on Porter street. Or on Dow."

"You got his digits?"

"Nah. We don't rock like that. I mean, he part of the team and all, but, well, you know how it go. Dem nigga's corporate. We floor level niggas, if you know what I mean." "A'ight. Good lookin' out, little homie…"

As Razor began to pull off, the youngster stopped him.

"Hey, hey…" he said leaning half his body out the window. "What you try'n'a do tho'… I got what you need."

Razor hit the brake. "Do what?" he said.

"I got it all… Purp', Ganny, Cat Piss, White Widow, we got it all. What you lookin' fo'?"

Razor smiled. "Is that right?"

"Fo' sho'. It's Diamond District, Fam'. We got it all."

"Is that right?" Razor said sarcastically.

"No doubt. Three for halves, five-fiddy for the whole. What's poppin'?"

"Shit, lemme get one."

"One? Of what, the Purp'?"

"Nah. Lemme check out that Cat Piss."

"The Cat Piss? Got cha right here…"

The youngster leaned in the window and came back out with a bag of dark green and orangish colored reefer in his hand. Razor raised the Mac-11. The youngsters eyes grew wide when he saw the gun.

"Oh, shit. Here, dawg. You can have it…"

Razor took the bag of reefer from the kid's hand and pointed the gun at his chest. "No, you can have it!" he said and squeezed the trigger. The bullets exploded against his chest catapulting him back through the window.

Razor put the car in gear and eased down the alley sniffing the bag of reefer. As soon as he reached the end of the alleyway, two youngsters holding semi-automatic handguns sprang out.

The first shot knocked Razor's driver-side rear-view mirror off, the second tore through his windshield.

"What the fuck? Young punks!" Razor said aloud as he threw his car in park and stepped out with his Mac-11 raised. He squeezed the trigger repeatedly, barely missing the mobile teens.

The youngsters were amateurs, no match for Razor and his skilled marksmanship. Razor ducked behind a large Dempsy dumpster and waited for the youngsters to get low on their bullets. After a combined twenty or so rounds from the youngsters, Razor popped up and aimed at the slim kid on his left.

Money shot! Razor thought as his hollow-point bullets struck the kid in his abdomen, sending him to the ground in a world of pain.

The second teen was a little more difficult to kill for Razor, but his inability to pace his rounds would result in ruin for him. Razor was counting shit rounds, zigzagging back and forth through the alleyway until the youngster's gun dry fired. That's when Razor closed in on him. The first of Razor's bullets struck the teen in his chest, instantly altering his white T-shirt to crimson; the second tore through his kneecap, sending him to the ground. Razor walked over and put two bullets into his head.

I'm only gettin' started… I won't rest until that muthafucka Dirty in the grave!

Chapter Twenty-Six
Interrogation Room 6

"So, Manny killed Pendergrass?" asked Steele.

"Yeah. Manny did it."

"And you're sure."

"Positive."

"You wouldn't be fucking with me, would you, Johnston? Because if you are I'll..."   "I'm not fuckin' wit' you, man. Manny killed that Fed."

"Hm," Steele said and lit a cigarette. "You know, your story sounds very plausible, but there's one thing that gets me a-thinking."

"What's that?" Pretty Tony responded nervously.

"Where the hell were you when all this happened?"

"I was around."

"And you expect me to believe that you witnessed *all* of this?"

"I mean..."

"Don't fuck with me, Johnston. I'm not the one. I'll have you getting bent over in the shower in Big Sandy, if you fuck around with me."

"Man, I'm... I'm not fuckin' around wit' you. Its offical. Everything I just told you."

"It better be. Now, go 'head... Finish the fucking story."

Chapter Twenty-Seven
Desperate Needs Call for Desperate Things

Dressed in nothing but a pair of silk pajama pants—and with two beautiful Brazilian women draped underneath either arm—Cashmere gazed up at the hand-painted Eduardo Ticci mural that covered the entire stretch of the twelve-foot-high ceiling in his bedroom. Usually it brought him solace and succor on the days he needed it, but on this particular day it did nothing but serve as a backdrop for his thoughts.

How the fuck could Manny do something so foolish? What the hell was he thinkin'? Did he even consider the heat he'd bring on us? Does he actually think he's gonna get away with killing a federal agent? What the hell got into him?

While Cashmere dialogued with himself, the phone rang. He looked over at Gwendlyn, a busty lingerie model from Rio. She reached over and grabbed the telephone from the nightstand.

"Hello?" she said in her thick accent. "Okay, here he is."

Cashmere rose from the bed and grabbed the phone. "Yeah."

"I see you takin' chickens to ya main coup now, huh?" said Manny. "What's up with that?"

Nigga we got way more problems than some bitches, Cashmere thought, but his lips produced, "Yeah, I needed a little R & R."

"Hm. I guess."

"Why, what's up? Everything cool?"

"Naw. We got more problems."

"More problems?" Cashmere asked. "More problems like what?"

"More problems like the nigga Razor bangin' four more of our little homies and shuttin' down two more spots."

"Fuck!" Cashmere said and rose from the bed. He walked out into the hallway and leaned over the eight-foot colonial balcony overlooking his living room. "You mean to tell me out of a hundred people can't nobody find this bitch?"

"Apparently. We loosin' a lot of paper, fuckin' wit' dis nigga… But look, I got a plan. Meet me at the crib on Jasper."

"When?" Cashmere asked.

"About an hour."

"An hour?"

"Yeah."

"Cool. See you then."

Cashmere gripped the cordless telephone and squeezed it like a boa constrictor. "If it ain't one thing it's another…"

$$$

Cashmere eased the Lexus over the small hump in the driveway at 422 Jasper and parked behind Manny's S600 Mercedes Benz. He silenced the engine, took a deep breath, and stepped out of the car. Cashmere was nervous as shit about meeting up with Manny. But he needed the meeting. Something had to be done.

Cashmere placed two firm raps against the front door and waited for Manny to appear. Manny cracked the door and peeked out. "Anybody follow you?" he asked.

"Naw," Cashmere said looking back over his own shoulder. "Not that I know of."

"Cool. Come in…"

The first thing Cashmere noticed when Manny opened the front door was the black AR-15 assault rifle in Manny's hands.

"Damn," Cashmere said as he locked the front door. "That nigga Razor got you spooked, huh?"

"Not just him. The Feds, D.P.D.. Shit, everybody!"

"And what's that supposed to do?" Cashmere asked with a nod towards the weapon. "You plan on shootin' it out?"

Manny nodded his head. "Yup. They'll neva take me alive."

Cashmere took a seat on the couch. "Fuck, Manny, how did we end up in this shit?"

"Trustin' the wrong niggas," Manny said. "Trustin' the wrong niggas…"

"Yeah, you're right. Probably should've never let that nigga Sonny in, huh? I always felt like somethin' wasn't right about that nigga."

"I know. But that shit would've never happened had I been on point."

"Don't be so hard on yourself, Manny. Shit happens, bro'. What's done is done. Now we gotta worry 'bout the future. Speakin' of the future, you got rid of the ten milly, right?"

Manny looked back at Cashmere from the center of the room. "Of course I did," he said as he continued to pace the room. "Tossed it in the pond behind old man Willa's crib. They'll neva find it back there."

Cashmere chuckled. "Remember how we used to hide our little stash back there?"

"Yeah," said Manny with a smile. "I remember you used to cry like a bitch when it was your turn to take it back. You'd always try to talk me into doing it."

"You got-damn right! Old man Willa is crazy as shit."

"Who you tellin'? You remember that time when he tried to beat me with the barrel of his shotgun for crossing through his lawn?" Manny said laughing. "Boy those were the times… Now look at us, stressin' out, loosin' hair 'n' shit, goin' everywhich way but the right way."

"Hey," said Cashmere. "You the one loosin' hair, nigga. Don't try to put that on me." Manny smiled. "You want a drink, dawg?" he asked.

"Nah, I'm cool."

"It's Louie. Black Pearl," Manny pointed out. "I know you ain't gon' pass that up."

"Yeah, what the fuck," said Manny as he rose to his feet and followed Manny to the kitchen.

Manny reached into the cupboard and grabbed two glasses.

"This shit is crazy, bruh," said Manny. "We got Feds on our back, a vigilante thug out killin' everybody with a fuckin' Diamond District chain or tattoo, and the worst part about it all is…"

While Manny poured the liquor into their glasses, Cashmere was easing the snub-nosed .38 revolver from his back pocket. The first shot caught Manny off guard. The second he saw coming. He fell to the ground and grabbed Cashmere's pant leg.

"Why?" he muttered with blood coming from his mouth. "Why bro'?"

Cashmere kicked his hand away. "You shouldn't have killed that Fed, Manny. It was selfish and irresponsible."

"But I… I… I did it for us, bro'."

"You did it for you, Manny. It was always for you," Cashmere said as he slowly lifted the gun and pointed it at Manny's head.

"Cashmere… Please don't… Please don't…"

"I love you, dawg," Cashmere said as he squeezed the trigger one last time.

After putting a bullet between Manny's eyes, Cashmere grabbed the bottle of liquor from the counter and took a giant gulp. Tears ran down his face as he looked down at his childhood friend. Cashmere wiped the liquor from his mouth, and the tears from his eyes, before heading out the front door with a chink in his armor. He loved his homeboy, but taking his life was something he felt he had to do.

$$$

After hopping old man Willa's rickety fence, Cashmere climbed into murky waters of his waist-deep pond and kicked around until he located the murder weapon. He then drove back to Jasper, planted the gun on Manny, and took the final step of his plan.

"911 opertator, whats your emergency?"

"I want to report a homicide," said Cashmere.

"And the address of the crime?"

"422 Jasper Street."

Chapter Twenty-Eight
A Wolf in Sheep's Clothing

Cashmere picked up the the local paper and read the front page.
Music Mogul/Cop Killer Found Dead.
Although Manny was a vital part of Diamond District, the outfit could survive without him. Sure, he was the company's lead artist, as well as the head financier of the team, but Cashmere could handle the task of CEO. After all, he had no choice but to do so, now. The future of Diamond District stood with Cashmere.

$$$

After Manny's funeral, Cashmere and the others decided to meet up at Mack Dame's pool hall, a local pub that served as their headquarters at one time. They ordered drinks, smoked tons of weed, and reminisced about their fallen brother. Manny meant a lot to the team.

Towards the end of the night, Cashmere made an announcement. With a glass of Cognac in one hand and a Newport in the other, Cashmere got the attention of everyone in the hall.

"Hey," he said over the crowd. "Hey! Listen up… Listen up real quick. I wanna give one last shot out to our nigga Manny Baby."

Everyone in the hall raised their glasses and bottle.

"We lost a good nigga the other day," Manny continued, "but we gon' strike back…"

"You got-damn right," chimmed in Product. "We gon' paint the city red 'bout our nigga."

"No doubt," Manny agreed. "and we ain't restin' 'till we get revenge."

"That's what the fuck I'm talkin' 'bout!" yelled Governor waving his pistol in the air. "Everybody gotta go!"

Cashmere looked over at Governor and smiled. "That's right," he said. "But we do shit the right way, the way it's supposed to be done. No more dead bodies. And no more problems with the law. We way smarter than that. Take care of your business and take care of it right."

Cashmere took a drag from his cigarette before continuing. "And another thing," he said, "I heard niggas been pointin' fingers, talkin' 'bout it was Dirty's fault that Manny is dead, and how they gon' do this and that to 'em, but fuck that. I ain't gon' stand for it." Cashmere reached out and put his arm around Dirty. "This is family right here. Ain't nobody gon' do shit to him. We all we got. Who we need ta be focusing our attention on is Razor, the person who took our nigga's life."

"That's what the fuck I'm talkin' 'bout!" yelled Product. "That nigga gotta go! My lil' bitch say she think he live with some chick named

Yvonne, on Reece Street."

"Oh yeah?" said Cashmere. "Reece, huh?"

"Um-hm," Product confirmed. "Three houses from the corner. In a white and blue house."

"Yeah," Fazion added. "I know a broad who say he be in Summit Courts, apartment 212."

"Good, good," said Cashmere. "Try both of 'em. Maybe one of you will get lucky." Cashmere turned to Dirty. "What about you? You down wit' hittin' his mama's crib again?"

Dirty paused for a second. "Why not? I ran through it once, I'll run through it again."

"Good. That's that then," declared Manny. "We don't sleep 'till that nigga dead, agreed?"

"Damn straight."

"Fuck yeah!"

"Let's do it."

Just as they were leaving the pool hall, Cashmere laid a hand on Dirty's shoulder. "Wait up," he said. "Look, bro'… I know niggas talkin' strong, but I ain't gon' stand for nobody doin' nothin' to you. I mean that. You're like family. You helped Diamond District get where we are today."

"Thanks, Cashmere," said Dirty. "I didn't mean for any of this shit to happen. It fucks me up everyday knowing that Manny got killed because some shit I done. Every day I look in the mirror, I think about killing that old lady and that little girl."

"Its cool, man. Don't even trip."

"No its not, Cash'. Had I never done it, Razor would've never been out for revenge and Manny would've still been here."

"Don't sweat it, man. What's done is done, bro'. Just do what you gotta do to make shit right, you hear me?"

Dirty dropped his head.

Cashmere patted him on the back. "Just take that nigga out. Everything is kosher. I promise."

Dirty slowly raised his head and looked Cashmere in the eyes.

"And clean up when you're done," Cashmere finished.

The two shook hands and headed for the front door.

"Oh, shit," said Cashmere and stopped in his tracks.

"What?" Dirty asked.

"I forgot to pay Dame for the drinks."

"I'll take care of it," Dirty said reaching into his pocket. "Its the least I could do."

"I got it. I gotta say a few words to Dame anyhow."

"You sure, man?" Dirty asked. "Because if you want I'll..."

"It's cool. Just go take care of ya business. I'll catch up with you later."

"Smooth. One love," Dirty said and shook Cashmere's hand.

"No doubt. One love."

As soon as Dirty made it out of Cashmere's eyesight, Cashmere reached into his pants pocket and pulled out his cell phone. He entered seven digits into its keypad and waited for the caller to answer.

"Hello? Toy? Yeah, it's Cashmere... It's goin' down tonight, baby. Yeah, yeah... He's comin' by himself... No, no, I promise. Just make sure you be careful... Um-hm. Yeah. Most definitely. Yup... Alright. Yeah. Just make sure to call me when its over, okay. Alright. I love you, too. Bye."

Chapter Nine
When the Guns Come Out

Product's source was correct; Razor did deal with a woman named Yvonne that lived on Reece Street, and he had been there within the last twenty-four hours. Product and Governor and two of their protégés posted up down the street and waited on Razor to show his face.

$$$

Razor had made it ten feet from Yvonne's front door when he sensed something wasn't right. He could feel it in the air. There was a black van parked on the opposite side of the street in front of the Wilson residence.

Razor gripped the handle on his Mac-11 tightly.

As soon as Razor made it to the street and placed his key into his car door, the sound of tires screeching filled the night. Razor raised the Mac-11 and aimed it at the approaching black van. Bullets pelted the windshield of the van, causing the driver to swerve and crash into a parked sedan.

The doors flew open and out jumped four men dressed in black attire.

The shooters were aggressive. They closed in on Razor, shooting with persistence, forcing him back towards Yvonne's front door. Razor scurried backwards—his Timberland boots flinging up mud from her lawn as he did so. He continuously fired the semi-automatic at them, but there were too many of them. He caught a bullet in the right leg sending him to the ground in front of Yvonne's door.

While the shooters pressed forward, Razor scrambled for his door key.

"Oh, shit!" he yelled as the bullets whizzed by his head. Razor opened the front door, and fell to the floor. He kicked the door shut and began rambling through his pockets for an extra clip. "Muffuckas think I'm a ho!" he said as he slammed the magazine into the butt of the gun. "Come get me muffackas!"

$$$

Governor and Product approached the front door with caution, Product on one side, Governor guarding the other.

"Hey," Governor whispered to the two youngsters accompanying them, one holding an AK-47 equipped with a hundred-round drum, the other a Tech-9. "You two, go round back… We gon' flush this nigga out!"

The two youngsters immediately took off around the house while Governor and Product stood at the front.

"We gotta make a move, bro'," said Governor. "The cops'll be here any minute."

Product took a deep breath. "Fuck it. Let's do it!" Product said and raised his rifle, an M-16 fitted with a five pound slide and an M-203 grenade launcher.

Product reached out and placed his hand on the door knob. He slowly gave it a twist and eased the front door open. A fleet of bullets spat from the door, one striking him in the shoulder, the other grazing Governor's face.

Product let out a loud "Urghhh!" and stumbled back into the lawn as Governor fired his .223 assault rifle through the front door like a mad man.

Product stumbled closer. "Move. Move dammit!" he yelled and fired a grenade round into the house.

"Boooooooom!"

The entire house lit up like a bolt of lighting shot through it. The windows shattered. Doors blew off hinges. And the coppery smell of blood filled the air.

Chapter Thirty
Hell Hath No Wrath Like a Woman Scorned

Dirty circled the block twice before pulling over and parking a block from Toy's house. He could've swore he saw the silhouette of a woman through the front window when be passed by the second time. He rushed to the next block over, shut off the engine, and sprinted towards the back of the house. When he reached the back door, he pulled out his semi-automatic pistol, screwed on the silencer, and twisted the door knob.

Unlocked? *Somethin' ain't right… Walk away Dirty… Walk away right now.*

But Dirty went against his better judgement.

This bitch gotta go, he thought. My life has been nothing but trouble since I met her. She gotta die tonight!

When Dirty entered the kitchen he found it unkempt. Pots and pans littered the sink area, and the waste can overflowed with garbage. Dirty passed through watchfully, the barrel of his weapon leading the way.

When he entered the well-lit living room, Dirty gripped his pistol a tad tighter.

I know my eyes didn't deceived me… I saw that bitch pass by that window, he thought as he tiptoed through the living room and down the narrow hallway that led to the two bedrooms in the back.

The first room to Dirty's left was the old ladies room. His heart raced as he eased open the door and crept inside. Suddenly, a shadow caught his eye. Dirty didn't think twice, he lifted his weapon and pulled the trigger, putting two half-dollar-sized holes into a terry-cloth bath robe hanging on the back of the closet door.

Sheeze. I thought it was—what was that?

The noise sounded as if it had come from the child's room.

I'ma get you when I catch you, bitch!

When Dirty reached the child's room, its door, just as the other, stood halfway ajar. Dirty eased it back with the barrel of his semi-automatic and crept into the room with caution.

 The only lighting inside the room came from a small Winnie-the-Pooh lamp that rested on a nightstand next to the child's bed. The room was dimly lit, certainly enough lighting to see that Toy wasn't in it. Dirty bent down and checked underneath the bed and inside the closet. No Toy.

The basement, Dirty said as he walked out of the room. *That's the only place that bitch can be… I know I saw her. I know it.*

Then suddenly, just as Dirty took another step out into the hallway, he felt a sharp pain against the back of his neck.

What the—

"Urgggh!"

He fell to the ground and everything faded black.

$$$

Toy was hiding behind her daughter's bedroom door with a metal baseball bat in her hands when Dirty entered. Her heart fluttered when he stepped in, but she knew panicking would only get her killed so she remained patient and waited for him to exit the bedroom. That's when she crept out from behind the bedroom door, raised the ball bat and swung it with all her might. The bat pinged against Dirty's head, and his legs crumbled beneath him. Toy took Dirty's gun, shoved it in her waistline and grabbed Dirty by the leg.

"You're coming with me…" she said.

$$\$\$\$$$

When Dirty awoke, he found that he'd been gagged and bound to the child's bed. He struggled to free himself but the ropes on his wrist and ankles were too tight.

Toy walked into the room.

"Don't bother," she said smiling at Dirty sadistically. "I tied 'em extra tight. I've waited on this day for months… You don't think I'd let you go that easily do you?"

Dirty took note of the the white latex gloves on her hands, and the large butcher knife in her hand.

"Mmmmmmm," he mumbled and struggled to free himself.

"It's a waist of energy, Hon'. Just lay back and chill. Let Mama take care of you…"

Blood covered Dirty's face and head, and his wrist bled from trying to free himself from the bindings.

"No, no," she said with a shake of her head. "And don't waste your breath, either, baby. You're gonna need it soon. I promise."

Toy removed Dirty's gun from the small of her back and sat the gun down next to his leg. Then the knife.

"Don't fight it, Boo," she said and ran her hand seductively down his chest towards his groin. "You like this, remember?"

Dirty squirmed as Toy unzipped his pants and pulled out his limp penis.

"Calm down, now… Calm down. Let Mama take care of you," she said in her most promising voice. "Um, there you go… I just need you to get it up for me… Get it up for Mama," she said as she stroked his penis with her hand.

Dirty struggled to both free himself and remain limp, but Toy was adamant.

"Oh," she said with a lick of her lips, "I see you're gonna make Mama work for it, huh?"

Toy jerked Dirty's penis several more times before leaning down and placing her mouth around it. She hummed and moaned and twirled her head on Dirty's cock until it rose to the occasion. Then she leaned back and smiled.

"Now, see… That wasn't that hard was it?" she asked with her hand stroking the tip of Dirty's penis. "I knew you'd like it. I knew it," she said reaching out for the kitchen knife. "But tell me if you like this!" she said and swung the knife.

Dirty screamed and yelled through the gag as blood squirted from his groin onto his face, neck, and chest.

"What? Huh?" Toy said with over seven inches of Dirty's penis in her hand. "I can't hear you. What did you say?"

Toy ripped the gag from Dirty's mouth and listened to him scream, taunted him with his own penis.

"You want this? Huh? You want it?" she asked waving the dark stretch of flesh about in his face.

"Ahhhhhhh! Ahhhhhhhhhhhhhh!" Dirty hollered.

"Aw, quit crying, you big baby. It's not that bad."

"Ahh! Ahhhhhhh!"

"Let me—let me shut you up before you wake the neighbors!" Toy said and shoved the severed penis into his mouth.

Dirty gagged and tried to spit it out, but Toy continued shoving it in his mouth. Finally she released and began slashing him in the chest and stomach with the knife.

Dirty was clinging to life.

$$$

Toy went overboard with Dirty, but he deserved it, in her eyes. He killed the only thing positive in her world, and for that she vowed to make his last days on Earth the worst, if she ever got the chance. Toy cut off Dirty's nipples, carved out his belly button, gouged out his eyes, and then sent a bullet through his forehead. It was gruesome, but he deserved every bit of it.

The moment just before she pulled the trigger was the best. Toy felt vindicated. She knew she'd never be able to get her loved ones back, but knowing that the person who took them away was rotting in the ground next to them was closure in itself.

Toy grabbed a picture off the wall in the hallway, tossed it in the bag with the rest of her belongings, and set the bag next to the front door. Then, she headed for the kitchen.

She lifted the upper deck of the gas stove and blew out all four pilot lights, closed the lid, and rotated all four burner knobs to *High.* From a utensil drawer near the sink, she removed a box of matches and a candle, which she carried into the front room.

Lighting the candle by the front door, she held it sideways to drip a few hot drops of wax on the coffee table next to the sofa, then set the base of the candle in the cooling wax, holding it only long enough for it to stand on its own. Then she picked up her bag and walked out, closing the door behind her.

Chapter Thirty-One
Interrogation Room Six

"Agent Steele scribbled on his tablet "So, that's it?"

"Yeah. That's everything," Pretty Tony assured.

"Nothing else you need to tell me? You wouldn't be leaving anything out, would you?"

"Of course not. I told you everything. Everything I know."

"Okay, but there's one more thing."

Pretty Tony sighed. "But I thought..."

"Hey!" Steele yelled, "Don't give me that bullshit. You've just sat here and ratted on every major pusher and gunslinger in the city. You, my friend, are in no position to bargain. I fucking own you."

"C'mon on, man... I thought we had a deal."

"Fuck your deal. Now either you do what the hell I tell you, or I'm sending that whore of a mother of yours up the river for life. You make the call."

There wasn't much thinking involved for Pretty Tony. He'd already broke the code, and he felt like shit doing so. He was all in.

"What is it?" Pretty Tony asked.

"Wait one moment," Steele said. He pecked at his Nextel. "Jefferies," he said over the chirp, "he's ready."

Approximately two-minutes later a slim, brown-skinned and seemingly uncoordinated African-American man entered the room with a brown shopping bag in hand.

"Agent Jefferies, meet Mr. Johnston—street name Pretty Tony. He's our newest recruit."

Jefferies nodded. "You must be big time, huh? Hope so. Got bills to pay, my man," said Jefferies as he tossed the black gym bag on the table.

"Whats that?" asked Pretty Tony

"What do you mean? It's dope," said Steele. "You work for us now. Its four ki's of ninety-percent-pure coke in that bag—much better than the stepped on bullshit that you're used to selling. The street value is somewhere between eighteen to twenty thousand per key, but seeing how we offer a dealer's license with our product, you'll pay twenty-two per."

"Twenty-two?"

"Yes. Twenty-two. But, you have a license to go and do as you please...with the exception of rape and murder. You have immunity on any other charges. You get jammed, just give me a call."

Pretty Tony shook his head. I should've never... I knew I'd regret this.

"So what will it be?"

Pretty stood and grabbed the bag from the table. "Give me twenty-four hours and I'll have your money."

"Cool," said Steele. He waited until Pretty Tony was halfway out the door and called out, "Hey Johnston? Don't forget to document those sales. Everything is done by the book on this one. No room for error…"

Chapter Thirty-Two

Watching You Watching Me
Club Horizon
(One month later)

It was Friday night, and a nice portion of the city of Dayton had flocked to Horizon to see Young Money/Cash Money and Diamond District perform. Candy-painted and kitted-up cars of all color and design covered the large parking lot, as scantily clad women pranced around the interior and exterior of the the club hoping to score some one-on-one time with the individuals performing that night.

Agent Steele watched the crowd, seeing little else but a bunch of black guys whooping and hollering on the stage, looking and sounding like fools. He was on the premises for one reason: to take down Diamond District. And what better way to de-throne them than to do it at one of the biggest shows of their entire career?

Shielded behind limo tint—in a black Dodge Magnum with twenty-four inch Asanti rims—Steele took note of the individuals going in and out of the club. He jotted down license plate numbers and brief descriptions of local drug dealers and felons, but his main priority was Diamond District. It was their day to pay the piper.

$$$

Agent Quinton Jefferies and twelve of his counterparts were spread out amongst the diverse crowd of partygoers inside of Club Horizon, waiting for the order.

"It's time," Agent Jefferies said to Agent Steele over this walkie-talkie.

"Take 'em!" ordered Steele. "Take 'em now!"

Upon Steele's order, Agent Jefferies and his team rushed Cashmere, Governor, and Product.

"F.B.I.!" the agents yelled and swarmed the stage. "Nobody move or we'll shoot!"

Jefferies walked up and slapped the cuffs on Cashmere. "We finally got your ass!" he said.

"Got me for what?"

"You're under arrest for federal drug and weapon charges."

"Federal drug and weapons charges? You can't..."

Agent Jefferies snatched Cashmere by the arm and dragged him off-stage.

Product and Governor were in tow, as well.

$$$

After Cashmere and the others from Diamond District were rounded up, Jefferies radioed back to Steele.

"Everything went as planned," Jefferies confirmed.

"Beautiful," Steele replied. "Take 'em down to interrogation. And Jefferies? Make sure you separate those bastards. Wouldn't want 'em getting smart on us, ya know?"

"Will do," Jefferies confirmed. "Wha'cha got going on later?"

"Meetin' up with a C.I. Cash is gettin' low."

"Cool. Hit me on my personal cell later. We'll have drinks."

"Will do."

$$$

After confirming that things went well with the roundup, Agent Steele lit a cigarette and leaned back on the car seat, waiting on his C.I. It was finally over. He'd managed to take down the assholes who killed his colleague.

Vindication.

After fifteen minutes and no sign from his C.I., Steele whipped out his cell. He tapped a few buttons and waited for an answer.

"Where the fuck are you, Johnston?" Steele blared into the phone.

"Not far," replied Pretty Tony. "Somethin' came up."

"Something came up? You were supposed to be here ten fucking minutes ago. I told you to be here at twelve on the dot, didn't I?"

"Yeah but..."

"But nothing!" Steele blasted. "You're fucking pushing it, Johnston. You're fucking pushing it. "

"Just calm down, man. I'm closer to you than you think."

"You better have your black ass here in the next five minutes or..."

$$$

While Steele was steadily rambling on, Pretty Tony was creeping up beside him. Steele didn't see the hit coming. The first bullet tore through the driver side window and struck Steele in the lower jaw, sending his chin across the dash. The next two shots ripped through his left temple.

Pretty Tony stuck the semi-automatic into the window of the sedan and emptied the clip into Steel's body.

"Don't nobody fuck wit' my family. Nobody!"

Pretty Tony snatched the bag of product from Steele's passenger seat, spit into the car, then bolted off down the alley...

"Guess I got the last laugh, huh cop? Rest in piss, bitch!"

Chapter Thirty-Three
Decisions, Decisions

Two deaths in one month. Gabby was taking it bad. She hadn't been to work in several weeks, and she'd missed so many meals that she was beginning to look sick. The pain wouldn't stop.

Gabby spent most of the time questioning God. Questions such as "Why were most of the good brothers in prison or in jail?" and, "Why does my son have to grow up without a father?" Each question solicited more questions, which solicited questions and more crying. Gabby cried utill she couldn't cry anymore, and when she could no longer produce tears, she cleaned. Gabby cleaned her home as if she were cleansing her soul while she did so.

Gabby had just finished cleaning out the refrigerator when she noticed a note from her cousin.

When did this get here? she wondered as she peeled the orange sticky rectangle-shaped piece of paper from the refrigerator.

The note read:

> *Gab', if you're reading this, it's*
> *obvious I let you down. Sorry*
> *Cuz, but karma's a bitch…*
> *Just know that I loved you, and*
> *that Sonny loved you.*
> *   Take care of yourself*
> *big Cousin..*
> *   With love and respect,*
> *   Desmond.*
> *   P.S. Don't get mad,*
> *but I left something in your*
> *guest room. Didn't know who*
> *else to trust.*

Gabby was both repulsed and amazed when she found the stash underneath her floorboard. She'd never seen so much money or drugs in her life.

What do I do with it? Gabby thought. *The money, I know I can keep. I'll have no problem with that. It's the drugs I'm worried about. What do I do with them? Do I give them away? Wait, no… If I give them away, I run the risk of having the recipient coming back and harming me and my son, thinking that there's more drugs. Do I destroy them? Or do I—wait! I know what to do. Let me call my ex-boyfriend, Pretty Tony. He'll know exactly what to do with it.*

Epilogue

As for Diamond District, the Fed's were lenient in sentencing. Cashmere and Governor were sentenced to two-hundred and forty months, Product received one hundred and twenty months—reduced time for his cooperation—and forty others were offered between sixty months and ninety months—substantial assistance imminent. And to date, they haven't named a suspect in Agent Steele's murder.

BLACK ROSE

BY:

Hector

Prologue

As a blackish-grey cloud loomed over the city, Death screeched through the streets like a rabid alley cat with a helpless mouse dangling in its mouth, its eyes yellowish in tint, its stomach completely empty, thirsty for the souls of men. He crept through the night, searching for those unlucky characters to cross his path, knowing then, and only then, he would become stronger and more feared once he fed. Then there'd be no stopping him, as there'd be no stopping Jason Rose now that they had turned him into a killing machine.

Jason pressed his lips tightly together and slowly removed his black leather gloves. The gloves were initially made for driving, but Jason had recently worn them to kill another dozen of his enemies. The gloves were now stained with blood and gunpowder residue—as were the other articles of clothing he was wearing. So Jason stripped down stark naked and threw all of the garments into a black trash bag. First went the gloves, then a black hoodie and sweatpants. Lastly, he tossed in his black, blood-soiled Timberland hiking boots and black toboggan. Afterward, Jason tied the bag shut and looped a snug knot at the top. He needed to burn the garments as soon as possible. No, he *had* to burn them as soon as possible. Too much was at stake to be making an error of that magnitude.

With the bag clutched tightly in his right hand, Jason sighed. He looked up at the ceiling and instantly felt a migraine coming on. So many things twirled around inside his head that he couldn't think straight; things he wished he could burn along with his clothing. Jason was truly at odds. He wished like hell that he could rid himself of his freshly stained heart, his diminished soul, and, most definitely, all the haunting images of his slain enemies burnished in his memory. Jason wished like hell he could just burn it all. But he knew he'd never be able to do that. He'd killed too many of Patel's men for that, and neither Patel, nor Jason's conscious, would let actions like that just slip away in the wind. Something *had* to come of what Jason had done. The only questions were *What?* and *When?*

As he stood in the center of the shabby and cramped room at the Duke Inn motel, Jason mentally searched for something—anything—that would take his mind off the bloodbath he'd just created on Wilshire Avenue—shifting him into a state of tranquility—but there was pretty much nothing. So Jason reached out for the only thing that would even begin to help him, a bottle of Jack Daniels. He broke the seal on the bottle of liquor and took a giant gulp. Years ago he would get queasy at the mere smell of liquor, but lately old man JD was Jason's only conduit towards escaping the pain. As Jason raised the bottle to his lips again, he began thinking about his son. He sat in that ragged motel room and thought back on how they'd play catch, how they'd go to see baseball games, and ultimately, their last prayer together.

Before Jason knew it, an hour had passed. He had gotten so wrapped up revisiting the past that it didn't occur to him that he had drunk nearly the entire pint of liquor. Jason raised the bottle and chugged what was left, sending drops of liquor gushing from the corners of his mouth all over his face. With the back of his hand he wiped at drops of intoxicating fluid, but they were entirely too quick. They scurried down his freshly-shaved chin like martyrs, nose-diving against his bare chest, crashing into the tattoo on the left chest plate. Jason slowly looked down to his chest, and immediately, a twinge of resentment ran through his entire body.

This tattoo, a beautiful and rather artistic form of expression, was pretty much all Jason had to remember his family by, and this was why he chose to have it placed over his heart. It consisted of a long-stemmed black rose with a banner twirling around the rose. The rose was as black as Death itself and the thorns that poked from its stem looked so sharp and pointed that they could pierce metal. Then there was the banner. The banner contrasted the grimness of the rose with its striking vitality and life-giving bright blue color. It swooped and swirled up and around the darkness of the rose, displaying the words *Rest In Peace Trish & Andreas* in fancy cursive lettering. The tattoo was awesome, and although it spoke volumes of both the love Jason possessed for his family, and the daily pain he felt from their deaths, it also highlighted the brevity of life for Jason. It seemed like just yesterday they were all having a wonderful time at Mount Zion's glory night, and then suddenly they were gone. Jason looked down at his tattoo for a couple more seconds, then he somberly raised his head towards the ceiling and whispered, "Why? Why, God?"

"Why me?" Jason asked, his voice raising a decibel with every word spoken. "Just tell me why? Why bless me with their lives, only to curse me with their death? Huh, God? Why? Tell me? Tell me why have you done this to me? Why? Answer me, damnit!" Jason yelled up at the ceiling as if he would actually get an answer. Of course Jason didn't get an answer that night. He seemed to never get an answer back from God, and as Jason thought, *I probably never will.* Just thinking about his wife and son brought Jason to tears. He cried. He cried hard. The tears poured out and ran down his face like a running faucet, and in no time Jason's entire face and chest were saturated.

While Jason was sitting on the edge of the bed sobbing away, a tall, busty white woman—a crack whore —and a short, Asian man—clearly a John—approached the room next door. The woman wore a cheap black mini-skirt, multi-colored halter-top, red high heels, and a stonewashed jean jacket. The man, on the other hand, was dressed in a crisp black suit, black shoes, and gleaming cufflinks. As the couple approached their motel room the Asian guy stalled near Jason's door.

Jason heard and felt the guy standing outside his room. Hell, he'd taken down more gangsters and trained killers over the past two weeks than the protagonist of an action movie. These types of instincts were beginning to become second-nature to him.

As soon as the Asian stopped in front of Jason's door to get a listen, Jason jumped up, snatched the handgun from the dresser, and lunged forward like a puma. With one rapid motion, Jason was now inches away from the Asian, with only the thin, paint-chipped door separating the two of them. With his gun to the peephole, Jason held his pistol steadily. His breathing was controlled. His finger dancing nervously on the trigger. Jason knew this day would come. He knew Bin Patel and his men would soon find him. His heart raced with anticipation, and just as he was about to pull the trigger, the woman spoke.

"C'mon now, baby," she whined, tugging at the Asian's arm. "Trust me, Hon'…you don't need none of that," the woman said suggestively. "Ol' Paula here is all you needs. Baby, I can suck a golf ball through a straw, and I bet cha ain't *no*body in there gon' top that." Jason pulled his gun from the door and looked through the peephole to see the

Asian turn and face the woman. She stuck out her tongue, wiggled her breast at him, and just before Jason lost his patience and opened the door to kill the two, the man gave in. He eyed the woman's huge breast, lustfully, and then the two chuckled, and off they went into their room.

The man didn't have a clue that he had been so near his demise. Neither did the woman. The reaper had gotten so close that he could've grabbed them both by their collars, and yet they hadn't suspected a thing. But Jason had recently realized the importance of acting out of impulse. He knew now that he had to think differently and be more watchful—that is, if he wanted to survive…if he wanted to complete his task. And doing so thus far had allowed him to successfully kill over forty of Patel's men, without, at least to his knowledge, ever being suspected of a single thing. Jason wouldn't get caught either. After all, Patel and his men hadn't been caught. They murdered his entire world that Thursday night, and yet no one had ever been so much as interrogated. If they could get away with murdering two kind, innocent people, surely Jason could get away with murdering a group of soulless miscreants. Patel and his men did have an extra edge over Jason—they were malicious and severely callous—but they had one thing Jason did not: The fear of death.

After killing the third member of their organization, Jason Rose had pretty much become numb to fear. He felt that he had nothing to lose, so taking their lives meant nothing to him. In fact, it sort of made him feel whole every time he killed one. But Jason knew he'd never be whole. Well, at least not until Bin Patel was sucking on worm soup.

Jason's disposable cellular phone vibrated loudly against the oak dresser beside him. It danced and lit up five times before he rose to answer it. He scooted to the edge of the bed and reached out for the phone. Jason didn't need to look at the caller I.D., for there was no mistaking who the caller was. He had only given the number to one person, Javier Manuel. Manuel was a lowlife drug dealer and human-smuggler who promised Jason pertinent information on Patel. He occasionally assisted Patel with smuggling large sums of cash back to Pakistan—money used to fuel Patel's criminal enterprise—but unfortunately for Patel, everything Manuel knew of him was about to be exchanged to Jason Rose for a large sum of Patel's own cash and heroin—cash and heroin that Jason seized from one of Patel's stash houses. Jason knew that it would soon come in handy. It was just a matter of time, and that time had finally come. Buzzzzzzz. Buzzzzzzz.

Jason pressed talk and spoke dryly into the receiver. "Yeah?"

"I found 'em," Manuel said with confidence.

"Where?" Jason answered back lackadaisically.

Manuel clicked his tongue against the roof of his mouth and chuckled. "Not so fast, hey…" he said, "…this is somethin' better done in person, no?"

Jason's silence spoke for him.

"I, I, I mean…" Manuel continued, "We've got a deal, man. You told me that..."

"Shut up," Jason spat. "I know what I said. Meet me tomorrow afternoon at, umm…at umm…Maribel's Pizza Parlor. You know the place?"

"I, I think so," Manuel answered, half sure. "It is… is it, across the street from the Duke Inn motel?"

Jason paused.

"Y-yeah, that's the place."

"Okay. What time?" asked Manuel.

Jason rubbed his face and exhaled deeply. "Around one p.m."

"I'll be there. Just make sure you bring the mon..."

Click!

Jason hung up the phone and began getting dressed. Things were almost over.

Also Available on Educated Thug Publications

❖Street Royalty 937 "Im So Sincere"

❖Street Royalty II 937 "Seven Takes Over"

❖The Incarcerated 7's Anthology

❖Everybody Dies But Not Everybody Lives

❖Blood Of A Gangsta Soul Of A Hustler

Coming Nov 2014

o Street Royalty III Build Or Destroy

o Pound 4 Pound

o The Incarcerated 7's Anthology II

ORDER FORM

Stonewall Entertainment Inc.
P.O. Box 1234
Dayton, OH, 45407

Name:

Address:

City/State:

Zip:

	Quantity

Title	Price
Omert	14.95
Trapstarz	14.95
Black Rose	COMING SOON!
Memoir of a Poetic Prisoner Part 1	COMING SOON!
Memoir of a Poetic Prisoner Part 2	COMING SOON!
Trapstarz 2: Still Trappin'	COMING SOON!
Omerta 2	COMING SOON!
Murda Dogg	COMING SOON!
Rico	COMING SOON!
P.O.L.O. (Players Only Live Once)	COMING SOON!

-

Life of a Hustler
COMING SOON!

-

Pimpin' the Pen
COMING SOON!

SHIPPING/HANDLING (via U.S

4.95

FORMS OF ACCEPTED PAYMENT:
Institutional Checks, Money Orders, and
PREPAID CREDIT CARDS ACCEPTED.

All mail orders take 5-7 Business Days to be delivered.

**ALSO AVAILABLE ON AMAZON.COM, BORDERS, BARNES &
NOBLE, BOOKS-A-MILLION, OR YOUR LOCAL BOOKSTORE!**